Look for More Titles by Cassandra Chandler

The Blades of Janus
PACK
PROGENITOR

The Department of Homeworld Security
Gray Card
Resident Alien
Business or Pleasure
Tied up in Customs
Entry Visa
Duration of Stay
Duel Citizenship
Invasive Species
Export Duty
COALITION RECKONING
Import Quarantine
Homeworld for the Holidays

The Forbidden Knights
FORBIDDEN INSTINCT

The Summer Park Psychics
WANDERING SOUL
WHISPERING HEARTS

LINGERING TOUCH

Other Works
CRAFTING A WRITER'S LIFE: Building a Foundation

Coming Soon

The Blades of Janus
PERIHELION

The Department of Homeworld Security
Nothing to Declare

Import Quarantine

The Department of Homeworld Security
Book Eleven

Cassandra Chandler

Copyright Page

This book is pure fiction. All characters, places, names, and events are products of the author's imagination or used solely in a fictitious manner. Any resemblance to any people, places, things, or events that have ever existed or will ever exist is entirely coincidental.

Import Quarantine
The Department of Homeworld Security, Book Eleven
Copyright © 2019 by Cassandra Chandler
Print ISBN: 978-1-945702-44-0
Digital ISBN: 978-1-945702-43-3
Edited by Evil Eye Editing

First eBook edition: March 2020
First print edition: March 2020
10 9 8 7 6 5 4 3 2 1

cassandra-chandler.com
P.O. Box 91
Mission, Kansas 66201

Dedication

For the furry friends who make our lives richer.

Don't miss out on any of the alien action.
Subscribe to Cassandra Chandler's newsletter at
cassandra-chandler.com!

Chapter One

A green blur filled Caitlin's vision. She blinked a few times, bringing the face of her clock into focus.

"Two o'clock in the morning," she mumbled. "Why am I awake at two o'clock in the morning?"

Someone pounded on her door, loud enough to make her bolt upright.

"That would do it," she said.

"Caitlin? Caitlin O'Rourke?" The voice echoing through her house was loud, male, and sounded desperate.

Caitlin jumped out of bed. The clothes she'd been wearing yesterday were piled on a chair next to her dresser. She pulled on her jeans and a T-shirt so she wasn't running around in her pajama shorts and tank top.

"Weapon. Weapon. What can I use as a weapon?" She spun around, looking for anything she could defend herself with in case he broke down the door.

"I need your help," he shouted.

She paused her frantic search.

If someone needed help badly enough to track her down in the middle of the night, something terrible must have happened. Or maybe something terrible was *about* to happen, just as soon as she opened the door.

If she went and talked to him, he might at least stop pounding on her door. At this rate, he would knock it down without even meaning to.

"Please," he yelled. "I need a doctor."

"Craaaap."

She grabbed her phone from her bedside table and ran to the door, stepping up on her tiptoes so she could see through the eyehole. The motion sensor light had tripped, and through the fish-eye lens, he looked...

Pretty cute, actually.

He had greenish-blue eyes, sandy brown hair—shorter on the sides than on the top—and a strong jaw and nose. Nice lips. Really nice lips. His arms were braced on either side of the doorframe and his shoulders were broad enough that he looked totally capable of knocking down her door.

"Wow, he is buff," Caitlin whispered.

He lifted his fist and hammered on the door again, hard enough to make the pictures on the walls shake. She yelped and jerked back.

"Caitlin O'Rourke!"

"I'm here," she yelled. "You can stop knocking."

His tone hadn't lost any of its urgency when he said, "I need your help."

"I'm not a doctor."

He went quiet.

She was about to look through the eyehole again when he said, "Brigid told me you were."

"Brigid," Caitlin murmured. "Of course."

Brigid, the quieter twin who somehow lived the more interesting life. Brigid, surrounded by celebrities that hired her to cook for them. Brigid, the valedictorian, who could do no wrong in their parents' eyes.

"I'm a veterinarian," Caitlin said.

"A what?"

"An *animal* doctor." Caitlin raised her voice so he could hear her clearly.

"That's what I need. Please, my cat needs help."

His cat?

She looked through the eyehole again.

The lens distorted his features, but she could still see the anguish in his expression. Why had Brigid sent him to Caitlin, though? Where was he even from?

He couldn't be local. The town was too small and Caitlin would definitely have noticed him.

"I need you to come with me," he said.

"Oh, no, no, no." She laughed as she spoke, her nerves getting the best of her—and making her speak loud enough for him to hear. Plus she was still looking through the eyehole, so her mouth was pointing right at the door.

"Why not?" he said. "Isn't it your job to help animals in need?"

"I have got to stop talking to myself," she hissed.

Hanging around animals all the time had firmly entrenched the bad habit.

Loudly, she said, "I'm not going somewhere in the middle of the night with some strange guy that I don't even know."

No matter how hot he is.

"I'll protect you. You have nothing to fear."

"That's exactly what someone who wanted to kidnap me would say."

He shook his head. "What does *kidnap* mean?"

"You're not helping your case. Everybody knows what *kidnap* means."

A few moments passed while he messed with his watch.

"That's... Cygnus X, that's awful," he said. "I don't want to kidnap you. I want you to come with me."

"And I don't want to come with you. Hence, *kidnapping.*"

"I'm not going to—" He pinched his eyes shut, then took a deep breath, expanding his already impressive chest. After holding his breath for a few seconds, he slowly let it out.

"Call Brigid," he said. "She knows you can trust me."

"Call Brigid," Caitlin mumbled in a mocking tone, but she was already dialing the number.

She didn't expect Brigid to answer, really. Her sister's latest client was keeping her busy. He'd moved her from Montana to Florida along with the rest of his household after only a couple of weeks in his employ. Apparently, Brigid was already indispensable.

The client must be a big deal. Brigid wasn't even allowed to tell Caitlin who she was working for.

"Caitlin?" Brigid answered before Caitlin had even heard the phone ring.

"Weird..." Caitlin mumbled.

"Are you okay?" Brigid said. "It's two o'clock in the morning where you are."

"I'm aware," Caitlin said. "But there's this huge guy pounding on my door. He says he knows you."

"Wait, what?"

Caitlin looked through the eyehole again. "Six-foot something, light brown hair, chiseled jaw...soulful blue eyes."

"Dane?"

Caitlin held the phone against her chest, and yelled, "Is your name Dane?"

"I'm Marq. With a 'Q'." His voice trailed off as he added, "Brigid said...people make assumptions."

Caitlin lifted the phone and said, "He says his name is Marq. *'With a Q'.*"

"Shit," Brigid said.

Caitlin perked up. Brigid never cursed. *Never.* This guy must be bad news.

Or *big* news. Like somehow involved with whatever secret celebrity Brigid was working for.

"Let me talk to him," Brigid said.

"Why?" Caitlin turned to lean her back against the door as they spoke. "So you can cut me out of the conversation?"

"This isn't the time—"

"No, it isn't. And it hasn't been for months now." Caitlin hated how rough her voice sounded. She hadn't realized how raw she was over this. "You're my sister. My twin. We don't have to share everything, but since you landed this new job, it's like you're shutting me out of your life."

"I'm sorry you feel that way," Brigid said. "And I get it. I really do. But there's more going on than you know."

"That's exactly my point!"

"Just, let me talk to him," Brigid said.

"You want me to open my door to this guy in the middle of the night? Because I was considering calling the police."

"Don't call the police!" Brigid nearly shouted.

"I see," Caitlin said. "So, I can trust him."

"Of course you can, but—"

"That's all I needed. Bye, sis."

Caitlin disconnected the call and quickly set her phone to *do not disturb*. She took a deep breath, then turned and opened the door. "Okay, so you need help with your...eep!"

Her gaze slowly rose from his booted feet, up along his muscular calves and past equally sculpted thighs. His T-shirt was tucked into his cargo shorts, showcasing his perfect waist. She could see the outline of his abs through the thin fabric.

His shirt clung to his chest, accenting strong pecs and shoulders she wanted to jump up and hang from. And his face...

Dear God, his face.

The chiseled jaw was even better than she'd imagined. Straight, strong nose. Lush, sculpted lips. Pensive brow, drawn together above those soulful eyes.

He was perfect. Impossibly perfect.

"I... Are you..." He stammered, then pointed behind himself. "Are you ready to go?"

"Hmm, what? Oh. Right." Caitlin shook herself. She had a patient who needed her help. "I need to grab a few things from my clinic."

She started by picking up her wallet and keys, then slipping into her sneakers before stepping out onto the porch. Instead of backing away to give her space, he just stood there, staring down at her. She leaned over to close and lock the door, doing her best not to bump into him— even though she really wanted to bump into him.

She slid her wallet into her back pocket, then gestured toward the path that led to her clinic.

"After you," she said, and not at all because she wanted to see if the back side of him was as gorgeous as the front.

He nodded curtly, then turned and headed down the path. Caitlin stood on the porch for a few moments, watching his long gait.

"Oh my God," she whispered. "It's just as gorgeous."

Chapter Two

"Are you coming?" Marq turned back to Caitlin, who stood just outside the door to her dwelling as if transfixed.

Too much time had passed. Meredith needed him.

He wanted to throw Caitlin over his shoulder and run to the ship, but that would be too similar to the "kidnapping" she'd been concerned about earlier. He held his panic at bay by focusing on his mission to bring Meredith help.

If Caitlin's sister, Brigid, was any indication of human behavior, ordering Caitlin to proceed wouldn't work. She wasn't like the soldiers assigned to his command—none of whom had ever seen an Earth animal before, let alone studied one.

They wouldn't know how to help Meredith. He needed Caitlin's cooperation.

Perhaps she was still nervous.

"I swear by the Solar Cross that I won't hurt you," he said.

Caitlin let out a short laugh, finally following him. "'The Solar Cross'? What does that mean?"

"It's what we call the star cluster that guides the way

from Earth to the Gamma Cygni system."

There was no point in trying to hide the truth from her. She would no doubt need a mindwipe after their encounter and would remember none of their interactions.

"Of course it is," Caitlin said. "How silly of me to forget. And that's important enough to swear by because...?"

"Sadr-4 is in Gamma Cygni." He shook his head. It was hard for him to remember that his homeworld—the entire Sadr system—had been obliterated. "At least, it used to be."

"Are you an astronomer or something?" she asked.

"Or something."

Caitlin paused, one dark eyebrow arched and her arms crossed over her large breasts. The lights from the building they were heading toward glinted in her eyes, slightly washing out their deep blue color. Her hair flowed over her shoulders and down her back in chestnut waves. For a moment, Marq felt a compulsion to run his fingers through the soft-looking strands.

Strange that she should prompt such a reaction when he'd never felt anything of the sort with her twin.

"This is getting weird again," Caitlin said.

"When was it weird before?"

She opened her mouth to reply, but a horrific noise drowned out her words. A large gray beast was charging toward her on four legs, a thick row of bristly spines running down the top of its neck. Long, thin appendages sprouted from its head on either side.

The only thing between Caitlin and the creature was a fence made of coarse natural cylinders. It was more blank space than substance.

"Look out," he yelled. He leaped between her and the beast, slapping his hand on his forearm.

Moons, his bracer was back on his ship, along with all the other weapons that might help him. He was on his own.

He widened his stance, fists raised as he prepared to face the thing.

"Wait a minute," Caitlin said. She slipped under Marq's arm, standing between him and the creature, and pressed her hands against his chest.

The moment she touched him, Marq felt a blast of energy rocket through his body. It was as if it grounded him into the earth and shot up to the stars above them. His skin tingled and heated, his ears started to ring. His muscles tightened, as did his groin.

What is this?

He wanted to look at her, to try to gauge if she was having a similar reaction, but didn't dare take his eyes off the beast in front of them. It stopped at the fence, opening a long, wide maw filled with enormous, blunt teeth. The horrific sound blared at them again.

"Bert," Caitlin yelled. "You're being rude."

The creature—Bert—screed in a breath, then bellowed

at them once more.

"Oh my God, donkey." Caitlin took her hands away from Marq to plant them on her hips as she stared defiantly at the beast.

It took an effort of will to keep from reaching for her. Marq's body remained attuned to her proximity, a vivid awareness thrumming through him.

"Seriously, you need to settle down," she said. "I know he's new, but it's okay. Brigid vouched for him."

Marq straightened. This thing was apparently Caitlin's guardian. He didn't want to have to fight it to take Caitlin with him, and he certainly didn't want it coming along to watch over her. Bert would fill most of the space in Marq's small transport ship. Marq needed to earn Bert's trust.

"I apologize for startling you," Marq said. "But as I have told Caitlin, I mean her no harm. Nor do I wish to harm you."

Bert shook its head, the blade-shaped appendages twitching and pointing toward Marq as if scanning him. They must be antennae.

Marq wished he had received more information about Earth's life forms, but none of the soldiers aboard the *Reckoning* were supposed to go planetside. He wasn't prepared for this. He knew there was an astounding amount of diversity on the planet, but would never have imagined anything like the creature before him.

A near-identical being, slightly smaller than the first,

emerged from a crude shelter near the building they'd been approaching. It crossed the fenced-in area and stopped at Bert's side.

"Why can't you be polite like Ernie?" Caitlin said.

Bert let out a series of snorts and grunts. For some reason, Marq's translator wasn't picking up the language.

"What's it saying?" Marq asked.

Caitlin narrowed her eyes at Marq. "Are you making fun of me?"

"Making fun?" He racked his brain, trying to understand what she meant. No part of this interaction had been fun. Well, except when she'd placed her hands on his chest. And even then, "fun" didn't seem a strong enough word for what he'd experienced.

She continued to glare at him for a moment, but then headed toward the structure in front of them. "Come on. I need a few things."

Apparently, Bert had given his approval. Marq eagerly followed Caitlin.

Metal clinked against metal as she picked the correct access tool to open the door to the building. It was a much more manual process than entering chambers aboard Marq's ship. Similarly, she had to flip a switch to illuminate the area once they were inside.

He followed her through the entry space into a smaller room off to their right. A desk protruded from one of the walls, and shelves and cabinets lined most of the others.

There were a few chairs that appeared comfortable, yet practical.

This must be her office. The room only had one window, which looked out into Bert and Ernie's enclosure.

Wait, were those companion animals? Like Meredith?

The fence around them was sort of like a cage, and that would explain why Marq's translator didn't work on the sounds Bert made. But Caitlin had spoken to Bert as if it could understand her. Then again, he'd been doing the same with Meredith of late.

Caitlin lifted a large black bag from one of the chairs and set it on her desk.

"It'll help if I know more about what's going on," she said.

"Dane brought me a cat a few weeks ago. Her name is Meredith."

"Hold on," Caitlin said. "Who is Dane? Because Brigid thought you were Dane when I described you."

"He's my brother. We're twins."

"Oh, like Brigid and I."

Caitlin smiled at Marq, and his heart made a palpable *thump* in his chest. His skin heated again, and more of that electric tingling spread through his body.

She hadn't even touched him. Why was he having this response?

He pushed his questions aside, focusing on his mission.

"Not really," he said. "But we do have identical

appearances."

Caitlin's eyebrows drew together over her nose. She was growing cautious of him again. He could now read the signs. If she was anything like Dane was with his patients, bringing her attention back to Meredith would divert her suspicions.

"Meredith has been listless the last few days," Marq said. "When I ended my duty shift today and went to check on her, I found—"

His throat tightened painfully. He swallowed, feeling as though something had lodged itself in his windpipe, then coughed to try to clear the pathway to speak.

This entire experiment had been a mistake.

Marq, along with many of his crew, had gone through a procedure that suppressed his emotions. Even so, discovering that he had a brother—and that they both had been conceived naturally, rather than genetically engineered—had been an enormous shock.

Marq had thought that recovering his emotions with his brother Dane's help would be a good thing. It was supposed to help Marq understand others. To enjoy life more fully. But he couldn't select which emotions he experienced.

This fear was not something he would wish on another.

Caitlin crossed over to him. She rested her hand on his elbow. This time, his body's reaction was muted—warmth spreading through him and helping him to relax and focus.

"Hey, it's okay," she said. "We're going to do everything

we can for Meredith. It's obvious that you love her very much."

The room tilted in Marq's perception. He felt as though the floor was rising up toward him, but realized Caitlin was simply helping him into a chair.

"Put your head between your knees and try to slow your breathing," Caitlin said. "You look like you're about to pass out."

He didn't understand why contorting his body would help, but did as she instructed. His skull stopped feeling quite so empty.

"This is what it feels like to love another life form?" he asked.

"'Life form'?" She laughed softly. "Sometimes. Our pets are family. And like family, they can bring us some of our greatest happiness and greatest anxiety."

He had felt happiness playing with Meredith. And he was certainly feeling anxious now.

Marq sat up straight, staring at the ceiling.

"It worked," he said.

"What worked?"

"Dane's treatment. He wanted me to learn how to love something. That's why he gave me Meredith."

"So, she's like a therapy cat or something?"

"Yes." Marq rubbed his chest. A dull ache filled him. "But this feeling… It hurts. It physically hurts."

"Well, yeah. Strong emotions can manifest in our

bodies."

Like the emotions—and reactions—he was having to Caitlin.

She reached out and gently stroked his hair. He closed his eyes so that he could focus on her touch, blocking out the fear that threatened to overwhelm him.

"I'm sure this isn't what your brother had in mind," she said. She picked up his hand and squeezed it. "But don't worry. We're going to figure this out."

Chapter Three

"Tell me more about Meredith," Caitlin said. "What makes you think she's sick?"

"I *know* she's sick."

"Okay." She walked back to her doctor's bag and started rummaging around in it, making sure her standard examination tools were there. She didn't have to make house calls often and wanted to be prepared. "But more information will help."

She crossed to her medicine cabinet and unlocked it while they spoke, then pulled out a few vials that could be helpful in a variety of circumstances, along with some syringes. She hesitated a moment before adding a potent tranquilizer.

Just in case Brigid is wrong about this guy.

After putting everything in her doctor's bag and relocking the cabinet, she said, "Have you noticed changes in her behavior lately? Sleep patterns? How much she eats?"

"Yes, I have." He sat up straighter. "She eats as much as always, and I'm careful to only give her as much as Dane instructed, though she often begs for more."

Caitlin snorted. "Don't they always?"

Marq plowed on. "She's been sleeping even more than usual. And she isn't as interested in her toys. But the strangest thing is how she's been dragging my clothing to the pallet where I sleep and making nests out of them."

Pallet? Why would he be sleeping on a pallet?

"She seems to prefer clothing that I've already worn," he said. "And when I went to check on her today, her breaths were heavy and rapid. I tried to remove her from her nest and she let out a sound of great unease."

"Oh boy…" Caitlin turned around. "I don't suppose she has a nice, round tummy, does she?"

"I… I suppose so," he said.

Caitlin let out a laugh. "It sounds to me like your cat is about to have kittens."

Marq swallowed hard, nodding.

"*Kittens*," he repeated. "Is it serious? Can you do anything about it?"

She burst out laughing. "I can find them good homes, once they're weaned."

"What does 'weaned' mean?"

"Okay, enough." She closed up her bag. "Did my sister put you up to this?"

Why had she even asked that? There was no way Brigid would ever do anything like this. Caitlin was the jokester of the pair. But this was too weird.

Maybe it was some stupid idea from the person Brigid was working for. Marq could be part of one of those reality shows where people played tricks on others. But Brigid wouldn't do that to anyone, least of all her sister.

Something else was going on.

"Are you ready to leave?" Marq rose to his full height. His very impressive full height, especially when he was standing so close to Caitlin's own five-foot-one inches.

She should be intimidated, but instead, her body lit up like it was having its very own fireworks show and Marq was the guest of honor. Her skin pebbled in goosebumps and tingling heat pooled between her legs.

"I'm… I'm not going anywhere," she said.

"But I need your help."

"No, you don't. There is no emergency. Your cat is going to have kittens. It happens all the time."

"I don't know what *kittens* are," he ground out. "I don't know what to do." He turned and let out an explosive breath, running his hands through his hair, then holding them on top of his head. "Dane never should have smuggled Meredith onto my ship."

"Your ship?"

Marq turned back to her. "Yes, my ship. No one on board knows what to do about kittens. Please, I need your help."

How could he keep a straight face while saying these outlandish lines? He seemed so earnest.

For a moment, she almost believed he *didn't* know what kittens were. Or donkeys, for that matter. It would explain his weird behavior with Bert earlier.

But that was just crazy.

"I'm sure Meredith is fine." Caitlin couldn't resist the urge to reassure him. "And she knows how to handle her kittens better than anyone."

Marq started tapping on his watch. "*Kittens*. What in the name of—"

The color leached out of his face as he stared at the display. It must be one of those smartphone watches.

"Offspring." His voice was a reverent whisper. "Meredith is about to have offspring."

He stared at Caitlin, eyes wide and jaw lax as if he was in shock.

She let out a sigh. "There's really nothing to worry about. Cats have kittens all the time. It's the most natural thing in the world."

His lips pulled into a huge smile, the skin around his eyes crinkling. "Kittens!"

She'd thought he was gorgeous before, in a brooding weirdo kind of way, but this…

His smile lit her up to her toes. She could barely catch her breath as heat flooded her belly and her knees became weak.

Marq let out a laugh. He swept her up in a huge hug, lifting her from the ground and spinning her around. She latched her legs around his waist so the momentum of his spin wouldn't make her accidentally kick anything in her office.

Part of her wanted to protest being picked up, but a bigger part was swept along in his joy. His laughter was so heartfelt, Caitlin couldn't help but join him.

He spun them till she was dizzy, laughing the whole time and hugging her tight. Finally, he stopped and pulled back to stare at her earnestly.

"How do I help Meredith take care of them?" he asked. "What do they need? Special food? More toys?"

"Marq." Caitlin rested her hand on his cheek. Wow, his skin was smooth.

He sucked in a breath, his gorgeous lips parting, inviting her to…

She caught herself as she started to lean toward him. What the heck was she thinking?

She cleared her throat, then said, "Meredith is going to be fine. And I bet the kittens will, too. What you described is perfectly healthy and normal."

"Will you please come with me to check on her and confirm this?"

Caitlin laughed and nodded. "Sure. But you'll have to let me down, first."

"I… If I lower you…" He stammered a bit, then said, "I'm having another physical manifestation of emotion."

"Do you need to sit down? I don't want to fall on you if

you pass out."

Although...

"It isn't due to concern for my cat," he said. He pinched his lips shut tight, pressing them into a line. His tanned skin flushed pink on his cheeks and neck.

"What is it then?"

"Your proximity."

"Oh."

She loosened her legs slightly, letting herself slide down in his arms a bit. He hissed in a breath through his teeth as she felt a hard ridge just beneath her bottom.

Holy crap.

"Oh!" Did her voice always sound so breathy and... smitten? She wasn't sure she cared at the moment.

The most gorgeous guy she'd ever seen, who adored his pet—*pets*, now—and wanted to take the best possible care of them, was unmistakably and undeniably as attracted to her as she was to him. At least, physically.

She'd take it. Heck, if she thought he wouldn't be too worried about waiting a little longer before checking on Meredith, she'd swipe all the stuff off her desk and let him take her right there.

"I have no intention of acting on my body's response to you," he said.

Well, that was an ice bath to her ego.

"Oh, you don't want to—" she began.

"No, I *do* want to. I mean, I would be open to

exploring…" He let out an exasperated breath. "I don't know the correct social protocols and don't wish to offend or frighten you."

Her brain seemed to lock up. Her body did the opposite.

She leaned in and kissed him.

At first, he froze, but then his arms tightened around her, pressing her close. He tilted his head, moving his lips against hers. Gentle at first, but then faster and firmer.

She opened herself to him and he immediately accepted the invitation, sliding his tongue in deep. His hands shifted to her ass, pressing her against his dick as he started walking toward her desk.

Maybe she'd get to live out that fantasy after all.

He'd taken a few steps when he stopped, breaking off the kiss and pulling back. "I can't," he said. "I didn't mean to—"

His eyes were clouded with lust. She was surprised she could string two thoughts together herself. They stared at each other for a moment, catching their breath.

Okay, that had been impulsive. Still, she didn't regret it.

"How about this," she said. "We go check on Meredith and make sure everyone's okay. And then we…explore our physical reactions to one another."

He smiled and nodded slowly. "Agreed."

Chapter Four

The fresh air outside of Caitlin's office served to clear Marq's head. He couldn't believe how carried away he'd become earlier. When she kissed him.

His dick was still hard. Remembering her lips on his sent tingling energy radiating out from his chest, filling him with warmth. He needed to pull himself together. They were heading for the *Reckoning* and Marq needed to be focused.

It was difficult, walking next to Caitlin, illuminating their path with a beam of light emanating from his watch.

He wanted to kiss her again—to touch her in some way. Perhaps he could reach out and hold her hand, as Dane and Brigid often did.

Marq wanted to ask Caitlin more questions than he could count. What kind of creatures were Bert and Ernie, and why did she talk to them as if they could understand her? For that matter, why did Marq speak that way to Meredith? As a veterinarian, Caitlin must have keen insight into such matters.

And more than that, he felt a curiosity toward *her* that

created an emotional ache in him almost as strong as his physical reaction. What had driven her to become a caretaker of animals? Why did she live in such an isolated location?

What was it like to grow up alongside her twin?

He couldn't sort out the mix of emotions churning within him. Dane would be able to help. But first, Marq needed to get Caitlin to his ship.

"That's some watch you have there," Caitlin said. "I've never heard of one with a flashlight function that strong. Or at all."

The device was a hybrid of Coalition and Earth technology. He didn't think explaining that would expedite their journey. He wanted to do whatever necessary to get to Meredith before her kittens arrived.

Kittens…

Marq was becoming accustomed to the warmth that filled him when he thought of Meredith as a mother. He was still adjusting to the fact that a natural birth was about to take place in his own quarters.

The genetic engineers took care of creating all life forms that the Coalition of Planets required. Even Marq and Dane had been raised in maturation chambers after their mother's unauthorized pregnancy had been detected.

Marq rubbed his chest, as if that could soothe the sense of sadness and loss that always accompanied thoughts of what should have been his family. The intensity of the emotions hadn't abated at all during Dane's treatment.

Before Meredith, Marq had spoken with Dane about whether the pain of restoring his emotions was worth enduring. He glanced over at Caitlin, a new warmth filling him, and better understood his brother's tenacity.

"Why are we walking into the desert?" she asked.

"My skimmer is nearby," he said.

"What's a skimmer?"

"A small transport vessel. Your dwelling is far removed from other settlements, which is fortunate. We also have a bit of darkness left to cover our departure."

"O...kay," Caitlin said. "So, are you with the military?"

"Yes."

"Are they going to let me on board your ship? I mean, don't I need a security clearance?"

"They will do as I say."

"That's very alpha of you," she murmured.

"I don't know what *alpha* means."

"It means in charge, I guess."

"That is apt. I'm their Commander."

"Wow. Cool." They walked a bit farther in silence, then Caitlin said, "And Brigid is working with you?"

"She is. She's now part of the Department of Homeworld Security."

"No wonder she's been so secretive. Wait, did you say *Homeworld*?"

"I did."

"Home*world*."

"Yes."

Caitlin halted. "If this is some kind of joke, I am not amused."

She sounded angry, but he didn't understand how he could have offended her.

"It is not my intention to amuse or upset you," he said. "But we do need to reach my ship as quickly as possible."

"Your ship." She narrowed her eyes, as if considering something. "It isn't actively deployed, is it? Because I'd feel a lot safer if it was on a base. I think."

"My ship isn't on a base," he said. "It *is* a base. We're in the process of building multiple operational headquarters which will all have a Sadirian military presence."

"Sadirian?"

"Yes. We're expanding our base in Florida and assessing additional terrestrial sites. We've also established mining and manufacturing domes in the Van de Graaff crater, as well as a colony site in Leibnitz. The main base will be the station under construction in LaGrange point L2."

Caitlin closed her eyes briefly and shook her head. "Wait, wait, wait. LaGrange what? And did you say *terrestrial*? Are some of these bases underwater or something?"

"No," he said.

"Oh."

She started to walk again and he gratefully followed.

"They're in space," he said.

"Okay. I'm out." Caitlin turned abruptly and headed back the way they had come.

Marq ran after her, grabbing her arm to stop her progress. She glared at him as balefully as an angered Lyrian. A chill shot down his spine.

"I may be small, but I have tranquilizers in my bag that could drop a donkey on its ass and I am not afraid to use them," she said. "And they're the fast-acting kind, too."

Marq let go of her arm. "Please, I need your help."

"The help you need is way beyond me."

He paused, considering her words. What help did he truly need?

The crushing fear he'd felt when he'd fled to Earth for assistance was gone. But now a new fear rose in him. Fear that Caitlin would turn away from him, that he would never get to kiss her again or be near her or learn the answers to any of his questions.

"Brigid told you to trust me," he said.

"Brigid doesn't know everything."

"I understand that you don't believe me. My skimmer is not far. When you see it, everything will make sense."

"I don't suppose a skimmer is a kind of spaceship."

He didn't know how to respond. If he confirmed her hypothesis, she might become more incensed. But he didn't want to lie to her.

"Fifty paces," he said. "Fifty paces is all I ask."

"Fifty paces deeper into the desert with a man I just met and who is stark-raving mad."

"I'm not raving."

She stared at him a few moments longer. Finally, she let out a huge breath and started to walk toward his skimmer again.

"Fine," she said. "But only because you're the one with the light and I don't want to get lost out here. And don't forget that tranq I mentioned."

He fell in step beside her, keeping the beam from his watch on the land ahead. When they were almost within range of the skimmer, he paused. One more step and it would decloak.

He turned toward her, and said, "I will return you to your dwelling if you insist."

"That's vaguely reassuring."

"But please, before you react, think of the kittens."

She laughed, but then quickly forced her scowl in place once more.

Reassured a bit, he stepped backward.

The scrub around them lit up as the ship illuminated the area, casting long shadows onto the sandy earth. Caitlin blinked against the sudden brightness, shielding her eyes.

Her mouth dropped open and a few half-strangled words came out. "This... What... I mean... It..."

"This is a standard skimmer craft," he said. "A small transport used for short-range journeys with minimal crew

—usually one or two soldiers."

"Soldiers."

"Sadirian soldiers."

"Sadirian…"

"Are you just going to repeat everything I say?"

"Give me a break, here," she yelled. "I'm standing in the desert in front of a freaking spaceship talking to a guy about… Wait a minute." She started to back away from him. "Are you a guy? Or are you some kind of alien?"

"I'm Sadirian."

"What does that mean?"

"It means I'm from Sadr-4."

"So you *are* an alien." She balked and shook her head, staring at the ship with wide eyes. "He can't be an alien. This is a trick. This is all part of an elaborate prank. It's not real."

"It is real, as is my need. Please, can we just go and check on Meredith and her kittens?"

"Her *kittens*?" Caitlin squealed. "You're still going on about *your cat*? If you even have a cat."

"I do. Just come aboard and I can show you."

"I'm not getting on that thing."

He scrambled, trying to think of a way to calm her, to help her understand. "You just said it isn't real. If it's not real, what is there to fear?"

"Getting into an enclosed space with a lunatic!"

"I'm not a… What even is a lunatic?"

"Why don't you ask your fancy space watch?" she spat.

"Because I would rather talk to you."

"Oh no. Don't you try to sweet talk me, with your soulful eyes and your ridiculous attractiveness. I'm not falling for it."

Ridiculous attractiveness?

If she was as drawn to him as he was to her, maybe there was still a chance he could get through to her without just picking her up and tossing her onto the ship. Seeing it in flight would surely convince her he was telling the truth.

But that really *would* be kidnapping her. The idea of forcing her to do anything was too close to his experiences with the Coalition before the war had begun. He wouldn't take away her choice.

Another part of him wondered if she actually already believed him and this was an emotional reaction to being faced with truths too big to process all at once. He probably should have considered that possibility before reaching out to her. But he'd been so panicked. Now, Caitlin seemed just as upset as he had been.

"Please, Caitlin," he said.

She shook her head.

The situation was beyond his experience. He didn't know how to address it. Deep in his abdomen, he felt as if his organs were sinking.

He had failed in his mission of getting an expert to assist with Meredith, but at least he knew what he was facing.

With the urgency removed, he could find another way to see to her care.

That didn't help with his other dilemma. He had also ruined his chance to get to know Caitlin better. The thought caused a physical ache in his chest.

The ache intensified as he thought back to their kiss and what he hadn't even realized it might mean for him. *Hope.*

Chapter Five

Marq was staring at her, his eyes gleaming in the lights from the ship behind him. Caitlin refused to feel guilty for not playing along.

It wasn't a ship. It was a trick. A prop.

Any minute now, a crew—a *film* crew—would walk out of it, sheepish that they couldn't pull one over on her. Caitlin tapped on her leg impatiently.

"Could you please give me a moment?" Marq said.

"A moment to do what?"

"I need to speak with Dane. Then I can escort you back to your dwelling."

"Fine."

She glared at his back as he walked up the ramp.

Damn, he had an amazing ass. And legs. And back.

She shook herself. Those thoughts were not helping.

Spaceships weren't real. Not like this one, anyway.

Marq's "skimmer" looked like something out of a sci-fi movie. It was crescent-shaped, like a croissant. A flying croissant. That's what she'd call it.

The outside was painted in a shiny black lacquer. Red,

green, and gold lights flickered here and there over its surface, in addition to the white lights beaming out of it in a solid line that bisected the upper and lower halves of the thing and lit up the desert as if it were noon.

It was held maybe eight feet off the ground on shiny silver legs. "Landing gear," no doubt. There was a small window that looked like it might be on a second level of the ship from what she could see from outside.

Not that she was thinking of going inside. Or curious at all.

"Flying croissant," she murmured, as she paced outside of Marq's spaceship, glancing at the ramp he'd used to enter it.

She wasn't being unreasonable. This was all insane.

Everybody knew what a donkey was. And about kittens.

Everybody from Earth.

"Stop it, Caitlin," she said.

She paused, staring at the light coming from the open hatch in the ship. Knowing that Marq was inside of it.

Marq, who had seemed so earnest and who her sister had vouched for.

Marq, who was a really great kisser.

Caitlin pulled out her phone and turned off the *do not disturb* setting.

"Crap," she whispered. No signal.

Marq had a signal. On his *spaceship*.

She looked back at the ramp.

"What am I doing?"

She slid her phone into her pocket as she approached the ramp, quickening her pace as she neared so she didn't chicken out. Voices drifted from the ship.

"I get that you're upset." The voice was similar to Marq's, but warmer. Caitlin crouched as she neared the end of the ramp, peering into the ship.

Marq was standing in front of a huge monitor. The face on the screen looked exactly like his, except not. Aside from the robust coat of stubble, the man on the monitor appeared more relaxed than Caitlin could ever imagine Marq being. Plus, his hair was longer, brushing his shoulders.

This must be Dane.

"I didn't know Meredith was pregnant," Dane said. "It honestly never crossed my mind to check."

"You're a doctor," Marq snapped. "You should have at least scanned her."

"I'm a *Sadirian* doctor, and honestly... I was carried away at the thought of finally finding a way to help restore this aspect of your emotions. Companion animals can bring out an amazing nurturing aspect in people. I mean, have you seen Ari with his cats?"

"Have you seen Rin with Ari's cats?" Marq said.

"That's not fair. Rin was traumatized."

"And it sounds like Marq may have been, too." A familiar voice broke into the conversation as an even more familiar face slid onto the screen. "Which wouldn't have happened, if you'd asked me before going forward with this cockamamie scheme."

"Brigid?" Caitlin whispered.

Brigid leaned closer to the screen. "It's going to be okay," she said. "We'll make sure Meredith and her kittens are healthy. But you have to figure out a way to convince my sister that this is all some kind of joke. I don't want her getting a mindwipe."

"I apologize for involving her," Marq said.

"I understand why you did, but you still need to fix this." There was Brigid and her ever-present damage control.

Wait… Why was Brigid with Dane in the wee hours of the morning? And standing really close to him—in her pajamas.

Caitlin ran the rest of the way onto the ship and jabbed her finger at the monitor. "Busted!"

Brigid's eyes widened and she leaped out of the screen's view.

"Just because I can't see you anymore doesn't mean I don't know that you're there," Caitlin yelled.

Brigid stepped back onto the screen. "Caitlin, you're really not supposed to be there."

"Where?" Caitlin said. "On a *spaceship*?"

Brigid's eyes narrowed a bit and her lips pressed into a thin line, but she didn't deny it.

Oh my God, I'm on a spaceship. Aliens are real and I totally made out with one.

Caitlin tried to mask her shock with a stern look, setting down her bag and crossing her arms so she could glare at Brigid properly.

"This is serious, Caitlin," Brigid said.

"No kidding, it's serious." Caitlin's voice had risen to nearly a screech. "I'm on a spaceship with a super-hot alien!"

Dane's eyebrows rose and he half-smiled, a deep dimple appearing on the right side of his face. Caitlin glanced over at Marq, wondering if he would have the same dimple if she could ever get him to smirk like that.

He was still glowering.

Dammit. Focus, Caitlin.

"Sounds like you two have similar tastes," Dane said.

Brigid and Caitlin both glared at him. He shivered and looked away.

"That is not fun in stereo," Dane said. He reached out to Brigid and pulled her closer. "This is good. I know you've been wanting to talk to your sister about all this."

"Now that Caitlin is aware of us, could you please tell her to go with me?" Marq said.

Caitlin turned her glare on him. "She's not the boss of me."

"I'm not telling my sister to sneak on board the *Reckoning*," Brigid said. "She hasn't been cleared yet and I do not want her getting a mindwipe."

"What's a mindwipe?" Caitlin said. She had a few ideas, but really, *really* hoped she was wrong.

Marq ignored her question. "She won't get a mindwipe. Commander Teisha is gone. The *Reckoning* is my ship now, and my crew will obey my orders."

"All of them?" Brigid said. "Can you truly guarantee my sister's safety?"

Marq's silence was ominous, but Caitlin didn't care. Her sister was hanging out with aliens—and had been for months. Caitlin was not about to be left behind.

"I'm going," Caitlin said.

Even if she didn't want to go for herself, the relief on Marq's face would have made it worthwhile. The furrow between his eyebrows lessened, and she could see his chest rise and fall as he took a deep breath and let it out.

"You don't know the danger involved," Brigid said.

"Neither did you," Marq said.

Brigid snapped at him. "That's different. Your crew abducted me."

"Abducted?" Caitlin took a step toward the screen, her arms dropping to her sides. "What happened? Are you okay? Where even are you?"

"I'm fine and I'm back on Earth in Florida, just like I told you." Brigid turned her glare back to Marq. "But I've been aboard the *Reckoning* and it was *not* a pleasant experience."

"My crew was only following the previous Commander's orders," Marq said. "I'm identifying those who are still loyal to her and removing them."

"'Identifying'." Brigid made air quotes with her fingers. "As in, 'you're still in the process of doing it.' I don't want my sister on the *Reckoning* while there are still soldiers aboard who are sympathetic to the High Council."

Marq turned toward Caitlin, a trace of the desperation she'd noticed the first time she saw him returning to his face. "I swear to you, I will keep you safe."

"Caitlin…" Brigid warned.

"You don't get to make this decision for me," Caitlin said. "I'm going."

Chapter Six

Until Caitlin said those words, Marq had felt like an invisible weight was crushing him. The moment she agreed to help, it lifted.

"You heard her," he said.

He ended the transmission before Dane and Brigid could respond, then turned back to Caitlin. Her eyes were wide as she stared at him. A nervous gaze.

Now that they were alone once more, Marq found himself uncertain of how to proceed. He didn't want her to change her mind.

"I promise I will keep you safe," he said.

"You don't have to keep saying that. In fact, it's starting to freak me out." She paused, then asked, "Is it really that dangerous on your ship?"

"Most of my crew is loyal to me or to our new leader. The few who remain focused on the past have no means to recreate it. They will share our perspective eventually. There is no way but forward for our people."

Unless they wished to let their ignorance lead them to destruction, as the High Council had done.

"I have a lot of catching up to do," Caitlin said. "But first, you need to get me to my patients."

Another palpable wave of relief swept through him. He felt his mouth twitch into a smile, the muscles in his cheeks stiff and unused to the movement.

Caitlin's gaze seemed to be locked on his lips. The skin of her neck reddened.

He felt his body lean toward her of its own accord, as though she was his personal source of gravity.

If he let himself go to her, he would kiss her again. He wouldn't want to stop.

He needed to get them to the *Reckoning*.

Forcing himself to turn toward the ship's command console, he said, "Agreed."

She stepped closer, further testing his control. "What are you doing?"

"Commencing systems checks in preparation for departure."

He entered the sequence and looked over his shoulder as the ramp slid into the ship and the hatch closed. Caitlin was staring at the console. It helped that her attention was diverted from him.

"Are these markings your ship's controls?" She pointed to the designs etched into the metal of the bulkhead.

"They are."

"How cool."

Marq tapped on another command sequence, opening

the storage compartment that contained his uniform, along with spares in several size ranges. "We'll draw less attention if we're in standard uniforms."

"Okay."

Caitlin crossed to the open compartment and pulled out one of the silver catsuits, as the Earthlings called them. He still didn't understand that reference, even after caring for a cat of his own. Perhaps Caitlin could explain it to him after Meredith and her kittens had been checked.

Marq pulled his T-shirt over his head and dropped it to the floor, then unlaced his boots and tugged them off, as well as his socks.

"Seriously?" Caitlin laughed as she held up one of the uniforms and turned to face him. "This is like something out of a B sci-fi movieeeeeee."

Her voice rose in pitch as she drew out the last word for some reason. She was staring at his chest, her eyes wide and mouth hanging open.

"Are you all right?" he asked, unfastening his shorts and pushing them to the ground, along with his undergarments.

Her eyes widened further, her eyebrows rising almost impossibly high on her forehead. Her gaze dropped to his groin and seemed to become frozen there.

"Caitlin?"

She didn't respond, but her face was now bright red, the color spilling down her neck and chest. Perhaps she was revisiting their conversation from earlier—about exploring their physical reactions to one another.

The thought of it caused his dick to twitch. Moons, it had only recently ceased being hard.

"You're... You're..." she stammered. "You're *naked*."

"It's a necessary preliminary step to donning my uniform."

"But... But..." She pointed at his groin.

"I told you earlier that I have a profound physiological response to your proximity."

"Yeah, that's...profound," she murmured, eyes wide and lips slightly parted. She shook her head as her gaze snapped to his. "So, you don't usually have this reaction when you're getting into uniform?"

"No. It would be extremely awkward for myself and my crew if that were so."

"Wait a minute. You all usually get naked together when you change clothes?"

"That makes it sound strange, but yes. Our ships and stations are necessarily small to utilize the least amount of resources. Most spaces are shared among crewmembers. But we also don't change very often. Our uniforms keep our bodies clean, in addition to providing us with protection and access to much of our technology."

That reminded him, he would need to deactivate most of the functions of her uniform's bracer. It would be too odd to have her walking around without it, yet much too dangerous for her to have full access to its technology.

The thought assisted with bringing his body back under control. That and the fact that she was no longer staring at him with that potent expression.

He took the opportunity to pull his own uniform and regulation undergarments from the storage compartment and put them on. He tightened the seals on his boots and snapped his bracer into place on his left forearm. After gathering his Earth clothes, he stuffed them in the storage unit.

"Do you require privacy to change your clothes?" he asked. "My attention will be diverted during the launch."

"Um, yeah." She was still staring at him, but without such a...hunger. "Privacy would be good. You can just turn toward the wall, since you'll be doing that anyway to work the controls, I guess. Just promise not to look."

It seemed an odd request, but one he could grant without difficulty. "Of course."

He turned to the command panel, quickly entering their course and beginning the launch sequence. Behind him, he could hear the soft susurration of her clothing as she dropped it to the ground. Suddenly, his promise didn't seem so easily kept.

If his body reacted so viscerally to her looking at his naked form, what would it be like for him to gaze on hers?

He clamped down on his curiosity. He had given his word.

And yet...

Merely the thought of looking at her was enough to cause his body to stir. He had to get this under control before they reached the ship.

The course was set, and he could feel the vibration of the ship's engines as they primed. He placed his hands on the wall and closed his eyes, trying to think of anything but Caitlin's warm lips and the fullness of her hips and breasts.

And failing.

She was close to the ideal size for Sadirians, but her soft, full shape was radically different than most of the women he'd been surrounded by. The genetic engineers wanted citizens who could navigate compact spaces— unlike Marq, with his abnormally large physique.

But then, he wasn't one of their products.

He reached up, pressing his hands and most of his forearms on the bulkhead above him. The ceiling was so close, if he jumped at all, he'd hit his head on it.

They'd be back on the *Reckoning* soon, and at least that ship had been designed to accommodate soldiers of various sizes. It was where the societal rejects were sent, after all. Anomalous results from mistakes or experiments.

"I could use some help here," Caitlin said. "These boots are weird."

"Is it acceptable for me to turn around?"

"Yes."

He turned to see her bent over, trying to seal the clasps of her boots. The skintight silver uniform strained against her ample bottom and hips. The sight made him want to reach for her, to feel those curves beneath his own hands, pull her close and…

"How do you— Oh, hey. I got it." She clicked the seals of her boots into place, then stood and ran her hands over her uniform, as if smoothing away nonexistent wrinkles. "How do I look?"

Like a star made flesh. Like the promising depths of space.

Her hair brushed past her shoulders in dark waves. The contrast with the silver fabric was mesmerizing. Again, he found himself wanting to touch her.

He cleared his throat, then turned back to the command panel. If he couldn't control his reaction, perhaps he could minimize the source of the stimulus.

"Adequate," he said.

Chapter Seven

Adequate? Wow, that was harsh. So much for "her proximity causing profound physiological reactions."

Marq looked stunning in his uniform. It stretched across his shoulders and hugged his ass. The wide belt looked ridiculous, but highlighted his narrow waist.

"I've initiated the launch sequence." He tapped different etchings on the chrome wall and ran his fingertips in intricate patterns over its surface.

A soft whirring filled the space and a panel slid away to reveal a window above the controls. The landscape outside was still illuminated by the lights from the ship, the cacti and brush casting long shadows away from them.

"I thought you would appreciate being able to see our departure," Marq said.

Caitlin stepped closer to get a better view. The ship rose from the ground quickly, the plants becoming blurs before fading from the reach of the ship's lights.

She didn't feel any change in their inertia, but the information her eyes fed to her was at such odds with what she was experiencing that she grew disoriented. Marq was suddenly at her back, his hands on her arms, holding her up.

"Thanks," she said.

"Are you all right? You looked like you were about to fall."

"I'm confused. I see us moving, but I don't feel it."

"The ship is creating its own gravity field. You shouldn't be able to detect any outward movement."

"That is so cool."

Like the view out the window.

Lights skittered by beneath them. They must be flying incredibly fast.

Then, suddenly, the lights below disappeared, to be replaced with a sky filled with more stars than she'd ever seen, even living on the edge of a town in the desert. They were also clearer, the space between them velvet black.

"Whoa," she whispered, leaning against Marq's chest.

A larger light source entered the screen. They were approaching the moon. *The moon.*

The reality of her amazing situation finally hit her. She was in an actual spaceship, outside of the Earth's atmosphere, traveling through space.

She felt a little woozy. Marq kept his gentle grip on her arms, silently supporting her as she took in the view.

Familiar features became strange as they neared the moon—the edges of craters that looked blurry from Earth standing out in stark relief. It was so bright from here, and there were many more craters than she realized—a history of impacts etched into its surface.

They sped across the gray-white landscape, flying low. It was like being in a movie with the most epic special effects.

"We're passing beyond our view of Earth now," he said.

He reached past her, wrapping one arm around her and hugging her close while the other worked the controls. A small screen appeared on the window, with a transparent image of Earth and weird symbols scrolling beside it.

"Are we going to the dark side of the moon?" she asked.

"Dark side?"

"That's what I've always heard it called. The side of the moon we never see."

"We call it the far side. Your moon is tidally locked to the Earth, so you only see one side of it, but it's still illuminated by Sol the same as any other object in your solar system."

"Sol?"

He hesitated for a moment. "That's the name of your sun."

"Oh." Crap, she should have known that. "I guess I need to learn more about astronomy if I'm going to be your people's veterinarian."

She felt as much as heard him suck in a breath. He rested his head against hers briefly.

"I would be honored to teach you," he said.

Her heart sped at the thought, at his voice close to her ear. She wanted to lift her arm and wrap it around his neck. Pull him closer for a kiss, and then—

Her fantasy stuttered to a stop, the view before her taking up all of her brainspace. She flung herself forward, hands on the window and face pressed close to the glass or…whatever it was.

"Oh my God!" she said.

Two enormous domes rose above a crater before them, made from a latticework of metal triangles filled with transparent material. She could see ships flying around inside the domes, and the tips of structures that disappeared below the moon's surface.

"Is that the colony you built?" she asked.

"That's the mining and manufacturing facility."

He stepped forward so he could stand next to her, his hands flying across the symbols on the wall. The skimmer rose, then circled the structures at an angle so that she could see into the shafts the domes covered.

Artificial lights ran along the walls on either side of the craters. The domes were connected at the center, sort of like a chunky number eight, and the pits they covered went down farther than she could see.

Spires rose from the center of each hole, with metal bridges linking them to each other and the side walls of the tunnels. Vehicles traveled across the bridges, kind of like trams, and elevators rose and descended on the sides.

"How long have you guys been here?" she asked.

"A couple of months." He tapped more commands and the skimmer turned, heading back over the lunar landscape.

"And you've done all of this in that short amount of time?"

"And more."

She glanced at him in time to catch his gentle smile. Her toes curled in her fancy silver boots.

Marq gestured back to the window, his smile deepening. When she turned around, her breath caught in her chest.

They were approaching another structure, but even at a distance, she could tell this one was different. It was filled with green. The skimmer circled the single, enormous dome, again angling so that she could see into it.

"This is our colony," he said. "It's called *Kindred*."

Gleaming silver and white buildings stood throughout the covered crater. The structures were wrapped in what looked like brown tree roots that gracefully spiraled around them. Window-like holes, lush plants, and even small trees adorned the roots.

The skimmer rose higher, revealing expanses of green surrounding the tall buildings. There were parks, bits of forest, and a small lake, as well as other structures scattered throughout.

"It's beautiful." Her throat felt tight. This was just...so much.

"Yes. It's the first settlement of its kind. We hope there

will be many more to follow."

"What makes it so special?"

"It's the first colony the Vegans have established in thousands of years," he said.

"Vayguns?"

"They're from the Vega system."

"Wait, V-E-G-A-N-S?"

"Yes."

She was quiet for a moment, then said, "You know, that could cause some confusion if people only saw it spelled out."

He smirked. "It already has, with fortuitous results. The Vegans were attracted by an Earthling who intended to advertise her restaurant's healthy cuisine by proclaiming 'Vegans Welcome'. That first contact has set events in motion that will benefit both of your people."

"Wow," she said. "That's kind of cool."

"This colony is the result of the alliance between Earth, the Antareans, and the Vegans. We assisted as well, but the Coalition never would have been able to make this much progress so quickly. Nor would our design have been so…"

"Spectacular?"

He let out a small chuckle. "Human."

She smirked and shook her head. "Well, I'm sure the Antareans and Vegans had a say. I mean this is amazing."

"And the diversity and creativity of Earthlings isn't?"

She'd never really thought of it that way.

"The structures were influenced by multiple cultures on your planet," Marq said. "The integration of natural and fabricated materials is based on the technology of the Vegan Life Ship."

"Wow." Caitlin tapped on the screen, pointing at one of the tallest structures. "I love how the trees and plants are growing on and around the buildings."

"Those are actually tunnels. They give the Antareans a feeling of home while also granting them access to the buildings. The dirt they're made from is an excellent substrate for the plants that provide food and oxygen for the colony. Once everything was put in place, the entire city became self-sufficient."

"That is so cool."

"It was Paige Sloan's idea. She's an environmental scientist from Earth who is working with the Coalition to restore the ecosystems of many of our worlds."

Caitlin shook her head, unable to form words as the magnitude of what she was witnessing settled in. Finally, she managed, "I'd like to meet her."

"Now that you've been made aware of our presence, you'll very likely get a chance."

With an effort, Caitlin turned away from the window to stare at Marq.

Okay, maybe not that much of an effort.

He was still looking at the city, his expression more relaxed than she'd ever seen. Light from the lunar surface reflected on his features, casting them in a glow softer than the lights from the ship.

She reached out and ran the backs of her fingers across his cheek. His eyelids drifted shut, his chest filling with a deep breath. When he opened his eyes, he was looking at her.

She'd seen that look a time or two. Usually before the best sex of her life.

Pure, raw hunger.

Whatever was going on with his communication style, he wanted her. And she wanted him, too.

Chapter Eight

Caitlin's gentle caress stirred the ache in Marq's chest once more—as well as other parts of his anatomy. He gripped her wrist as she started to pull her hand away, pressing her palm to his cheek and holding it there.

Her lips parted. He couldn't resist.

Closing the space between them, he pulled her up against his body and leaned down to kiss her. Her lips were warm and soft. Softer than anything he'd ever felt.

She moaned as he shifted his mouth across hers, tasting her, letting her warmth soak into him. He'd been able to explore her the last time they kissed. He wanted that intimacy again.

He ran his tongue across her lips, questioning. Once more, she opened herself to him. His dick throbbed with longing as he slid his tongue into her, relishing everything she had to give.

She wrapped her arms around his shoulders, leaping up and gripping his waist with her legs, as she'd done back at the clinic. The context was so very different this time.

With better access, she returned his kiss with ardor,

burrowing her fingers through his hair, nipping at his lips. He gripped her backside, pressing her close, grinding his erection against her core.

This was bliss. Better than any time he'd used *Coupling* —the drug used by the Coalition to manage their population's biological needs. It couldn't compare at all to this—to *feeling* Caitlin—experiencing every shiver and tantalizing caress. He'd never been so attuned to someone else, or to his own body.

He wanted more.

Pressing her up against the wall, he thrust against her, losing touch with all reason and thought. There was only sensation and pleasure.

He ran his lips along her jaw, kissing a path to her neck and tracing his teeth over her skin. She gasped, clutching at his back.

"Oh God, Marq."

Her words spurred him on. He could feel a throbbing pressure building in his groin. Her breath caught in spurts as her fingers dug into his muscles.

How could anything feel so good?

Just when he thought their worlds were about to collapse and remake themselves, the communications alert went off.

Caitlin stiffened, gasping for breath. He was panting as well.

The communications controls were too far for him to reach. He let her slide to her feet, holding her gaze the entire time.

The pinging persisted, grating on senses that were already saturated.

"That sounds important," she said.

He let out an exasperated breath, surprising himself in how much it resembled a growl. Caitlin grinned, her eyes heavy-lidded.

Marq stepped away, then slammed the side of his fist onto the communications control.

"What?" he barked.

"Commander," a smooth female voice said. "Is everything all right?"

Sorca.

His chief of security.

He forced his voice to sound calmer. "Yes."

"You changed course," Sorca said.

"I'm conducting a visual inspection of our sites." It was a plausible enough explanation, but he wasn't certain Sorca would believe him. She was head of his security for a reason.

"I trust you're finding everything in order." Sorca often sounded as though she knew more than she was revealing. This was one of those times, and it irritated Marq even more.

"Affirmative," he said.

"Shall I inform *Outreach* that they can expect a flyby?" Sorca asked. "I wouldn't want any of my team to think you're a saboteur and embody trigger-glee."

"I believe the expression is 'become trigger-happy'. Proceed with notifying *Outreach*." Marq tapped the control to end the transmission.

"Who was that?" Caitlin had her arms crossed, one hip jutting out and her head angled to the side. The same posture that she'd held when she'd been upset with him earlier.

"That was Sorca. She's in charge of security on the *Reckoning*."

Caitlin kept staring at him, as if she expected additional information.

"And...she's a Cygnian-Sadirian hybrid," he said.

"Like I know what that is."

"Her Sadirian DNA has been combined with another sentient species. It is—was—a very rare occurrence, making her invaluable to the Coalition fleet." And the High Council, before they'd been assassinated. "We'll need to be cautious around her."

"Why, because she'll be jealous?"

"Do you mean romantic jealousy?" The side of his lips pulled up again, deeper this time. He wondered if this was his first true smirk. "It is my understanding that for one to experience that particular emotion, they must be involved in a relationship. And Sorca and I are not involved beyond our duty assignments."

Caitlin shrugged and looked away. Marq stepped closer

to her, resting his hands on her hips, as he'd longed to do. He flexed his fingers, relishing the fullness of her body.

Her mouth fell open a bit and she glanced up at him. Her breath quickened and a pink flush spread over her cheeks.

"Are *you* experiencing jealousy, Caitlin?"

She shook her head, then stared up at him, holding his gaze with burning eyes. "Maybe."

"Does that mean we're in a relationship?"

Her lips twitched—first pulling into a smile, then pursing as if she was trying to fight it. She stepped closer to him and wrapped her hands around his shoulders once more.

"It seems kind of fast for that," she said. "But then, I am the jealous type." She shrugged again. "I'm working on it."

"This is still part of us exploring each other," he said. "And it is uncharted territory for me."

Caitlin laughed. "Says the guy flying the Earthling past his moon bases."

He echoed her laugh, the sound becoming familiar. He had a feeling he would need to grow accustomed to it while he was with her.

"The only reason I mentioned Sorca's uniqueness is to let you know that her senses are more acute than most Sadirians'. Once we reach the *Reckoning*, we'll need to be cautious with her or she may detect that you're an Earthling."

"I'll keep all that in mind in case I have to fight her for

you."

The thought chilled him. "That's not something to joke about. She's our best fighter—the strongest and fastest soldier in the fleet. Cygnians are a warrior race and Sorca follows their customs in that regard. The only person to ever best her in battle is her bondmate, Eric Peterson."

A little furrow appeared between Caitlin's brows. Marq found himself wanting to kiss it, but held himself back.

"That sounds like an Earth name," she said.

"It is."

"What's a bondmate, then?"

"It's most closely akin to spouses in your culture. Eric is part of the Department of Homeworld Security—the group that is our point of contact for all things involving Earth, like obtaining permission to build the moon bases and *Outreach*."

"Sorca mentioned *Outreach* as well. Is that another colony?"

"It's the space station."

"You guys sure are building a lot of stuff out here. Aren't you afraid we're going to notice it?"

"Earthlings are very close to being able to colonize the moon, and we're having to work around various satellites. With our cloaking fields, sensors, and ability to override Earth's technology feeds, we should be able to remain secret until it's time to let everyone know of our presence."

"When will that be?"

When the war is over?

He opened his mouth to speak, but thought better of it. He didn't wish to frighten her.

"Soon," he said. He hoped he spoke the truth.

Chapter Nine

Caitlin had finally managed to rouse the willpower to let go of Marq so he could change their course yet again. His crew must think it weird how long they'd circled *Kindred* while they were talking. Marq didn't seem bothered by it.

The ship was climbing again. This time, as the surface of the moon fell away to be replaced with stars, the window was taken up almost entirely with an enormous structure. Skeletal rings of metal wrapped around a central spike, giving her an idea of what it would look like when it was done.

"Oh wow," she said.

Smaller ships buzzed about the proto-station, lights sparking in some places as giant sections of metal were fused together. A blocky shuttle passed them, heading in the direction of the moon bases.

"This is incredible," Caitlin said.

She turned to Marq when he didn't respond. The deep furrows were back between his brows and he was staring intently at the smaller screen superimposed on the window. His lips were pulled in a deep frown.

"Is something wrong?" she asked.

He shook his head. "Sorca must have told Nika I was conducting inspections. She's sent me a report on operations. We're falling behind on fabrication of key components we're going to need to keep construction on schedule. Nika will wish to speak with me as soon as we board my ship."

"Is your ship as impressive as the moon bases and space station?"

"See for yourself."

His frown slowly transformed into a smile as he stepped behind her and turned her to face the window again, her back against his chest. This time, when he wrapped both arms around her and held her close, it had nothing to do with trying to keep her upright.

A thrill skittered over her at his closeness and feeling the strength of his embrace. She could definitely get used to this.

The skimmer circled the space station only once. Another structure started to come into view—a huge ship, nearly half the size of the space station.

It was spearlike, long and sleek, with a sharp front and broader back-end. Unless what she thought was the back end was actually the front. It was hard to tell with it hanging there in space.

The design looked almost aerodynamic, but she couldn't imagine a ship that huge flying through any kind of atmosphere. There were also large protrusions on every surface, with openings that faced forward, backward, and toward both sides. Spinning circular lights within each reminded her of the chambers of the big machine guns she'd seen mounted on helicopters in a couple of movies.

"That's, um…" she began. "That's a heck of a lot of guns."

"The *Reckoning* is the ship responsible for enforcing Coalition law, along with her sister ship, the *Arbiter*."

Those names didn't sound very peaceful.

"Do you have to do that a lot?" she asked. "Enforce law?"

He didn't respond, but she felt his breath hitch.

"If this ship brings the consequences, I don't understand how anyone would dare to try to break your laws," she said. "I mean, who could stand up to this?"

"It is…possible."

"That sounds kind of scary."

Marq hugged her tighter, resting his chin on the top of her head. "I didn't wish to speak of this."

"*This* being whatever was making my sister so nervous about me going aboard your ship."

"Yes."

She gave him a few more moments, then said, "Are you going to tell me?"

Marq let out a long breath. "Until recently, the Coalition was the greatest technological power in the galaxy."

"The galaxy? Wow."

"We had an enormous fleet, military bases at strategic locations, and the loyalty of every planet, domeworld, and space station inhabited by sentients."

"Or so you thought."

"We knew there were those who wished for independence. Otherwise, the fleet wouldn't be necessary. What we didn't know is that they had formed what they call the Tau Centauran Assembly—and somehow obtained technology that far surpassed our own."

"That doesn't sound good."

"In a way…they may have created a path for all of us to be free."

She turned in his arms so that she could see his expression as he spoke. This sounded like the kind of talk that could get a soldier into trouble.

"Are you supposed to be saying this?" She looked around the ship, at all the controls and technology she didn't understand. "I mean, can't someone be listening in?"

Marq shook his head. "The High Council might have done such a thing, but I have more faith in our current leaders."

"Are they that assembly that wanted independence?"

"No, not at all."

"It's just… You made it seem like maybe they're the good guys."

"They are most assuredly not the good guys. But their

first act of aggression was to destroy our High Council."

"Okay. Definitely bad guys." Then again, Marq didn't seem that broken up about it.

He shook his head. "Actually, in comparing the acts of the High Council against that of the Tau Centauran Assembly…" A grim look crossed his features, the furrow between his brow deepening. "Their deaths were a blessing."

His words chilled her. "How can you say that?"

"Because I know of the crimes of the High Council— more than almost any other Sadirian. They cared only for themselves and for maintaining their power and access to resources. They've done terrible things, Caitlin. Unspeakable things."

His eyes glistened as he spoke and his voice took on a more gravelly tone.

She kept her voice gentle. "How can anyone on your ship be loyal to them then?"

"Not everyone is aware of the previous situation," he said. "If word were to spread of some of their atrocities, there would be chaos and despair."

"And nobody wants that."

The room seemed to be spinning a bit. Brigid was right —not that Caitlin would ever admit it. There was so much more going on here than Caitlin had realized. This was definitely turning into the most complex "routine checkup" she'd ever done.

"I think I need to sit down for a minute." She looked around the ship, but the area they were standing in was empty. "All this advanced technology and you guys don't have chairs?"

"Not on skimmers." At her questioning look, he elaborated. "Small ships like this one are meant for only short-term travel. There's a resting area above, though, if you'd like to lie down."

"I'm okay," she said. "I just need a minute."

He held her closer against his chest. The feel of his arms around her grounded her more than the artificial gravity of the ship.

"I didn't wish to burden you with this knowledge," he said.

"It's my galaxy, too. I'd rather know what's going on. It's just a lot to absorb."

"You're handling all of this magnificently. We'll be on the *Reckoning* soon, and my quarters have ample seating. You'll be able to rest then."

She laughed a bit and looked up at him. "After I check on my patients."

He shrugged sheepishly. "If you are able to. I'll be reassured once I've seen Meredith with my own eyes. The examination can wait until you're feeling strong enough."

"I'm strong enough." She tilted her chin up and glared at him.

Marq smiled and nodded. "That you are."

She looked over her shoulder at the ship they were approaching. One of the small, box-shaped vessels flew out from a large opening that spanned the underside of the ship, turning toward *Outreach*. The skimmer headed for the hangar.

"Your heart is pounding," Marq said.

Caitlin swallowed past a lump in her throat, willing herself to calm. "Does your suit have sensors that tell you that?"

"I can feel it through our bodies."

He leaned back and rested his hand on her chest above her heart. Which also meant it was on her breasts.

That only made her heart pound harder. Lightning arced through her nerves, her skin tingling and heat firing like a furnace in her belly.

He probably didn't know what putting his hand there meant for an Earthling. Nudity wasn't a taboo for his people, and maybe touching that particular part of her anatomy wasn't a big deal, either.

Still, she couldn't stop herself from imagining him sliding his hand into her suit and cupping her breast. She would kiss him again. They'd slip out of their uniforms and...

Light flooded the ship as they entered the hangar, burning away her fantasy. It had been so much more enjoyable than the fears that suddenly plagued her.

This was a badass alien spaceship with a scary name and

whose purpose was to enforce laws set by what sounded like an evil regime that had been displaced by a faction of people—of *aliens*—whose motives she knew next to nothing about. She had no idea what would happen to her here.

But her sister had been aboard, and she was fine.

Marq cupped Caitlin's chin, turning her gaze toward his.

"I am the Commander of the *Reckoning*," he said. "I swear to you, I will keep you safe. Can you trust me?"

She took a deep breath, then nodded. "I can."

Chapter Ten

"You'll need to put your hair up." Marq finished making the last adjustments to Caitlin's bracer, locking down its functions. They were nearly ready to disembark. "Our helmets automatically deploy in the event of depressurization, and you don't want anything in the way if it does."

"Depressurization, huh? Does that happen often?" Caitlin was smiling, but her voice trembled.

"Not at all," he said. "But it's regulation to wear our hair in ways that won't interfere with our uniform. You'll stand out less if your hair is up."

She crossed to the large black bag she'd brought with her and started going through its contents, then stood when she'd found a tie. As she reached behind her head to pull her hair into place, the material of her uniform strained against her breasts.

She was going to be conspicuous enough as it was.

And if he kept staring at her chest, he was going to become conspicuous himself. Already, he felt his body stirring. He quickly turned away, finalizing their arrival procedures.

The skimmer had landed in the main hangar bay without incident. A soft orange glow covered the viewport.

"What's with that light?" she asked.

"Decon procedures. The outer hull is being purged of random radiation and any contaminants it might have picked up on Earth."

"I guess that makes sense. Do we need to be decontaminated, too?"

"Our uniforms take care of that."

"What if you pick up something on Earth? A germ or a sickness or something internal?"

"I and my crew have been inoculated against any pathogens that might do us harm. We've also been purged of anything that might be harmful to Earth's life forms."

"Good to know," she murmured.

She finished with her hair, putting it in a ponytail high on the back of her head and looping the long strands into the band so that it was gathered together in something akin to a loose bun. He missed seeing it flowing around her shoulders and rippling down her back.

She tilted her head at him. "Is it okay?"

"Yes, it's—"

"Adequate?" She smirked.

He had a feeling he was missing something, but couldn't figure out what it was. Giving up on that particular mystery, he said, "I can help you with your bag."

"I've got it."

They both reached for the handle, their hands colliding. They rose at the same time, standing close and still holding on to the bag.

"I appreciate your help," he said.

She arched an eyebrow at him. "It's going to cost you."

His heart felt as though it plummeted through his stomach and into his belly. Earth was still dominated by commerce-based cultures. What would she even find of value? He was a soldier, not a merchant. Life on his ship was all he'd known. This was yet more new territory for him.

"I will see to it that you're compensated for your time." He relinquished his hold on her bag and stepped back. "I have ample resources with which to trade."

"I don't want your resources. Well…" Her gaze slid over his body like a caress, and her smile broadened.

His body responded once more, energy pulsing through him, heat flooding his abdomen.

"I want answers," she said. "A lot of them."

That, he could do.

He nodded, and said, "I will tell you everything I can, once we reach my quarters and you've had a chance to examine Meredith. It's too dangerous to discuss these matters in front of my crew."

"So you *can* get in trouble for bringing an Earthling aboard. I thought 'your crew will do as you say'." She lowered her voice and scowled as she repeated his words from earlier. He felt a strange urge to laugh at her imitation, but stifled it.

"They will follow my commands," he said. "But I'm not the highest authority in the Coalition. There could be consequences if you're discovered."

Consequences he was finding less and less acceptable.

"Who's in charge now that the High Council is gone?" she asked.

"General Serath. On Earth, he's known as Adam Smith."

"Adam Smith? Seriously? That's the best you could do?"

"I don't understand."

"That name sounds really fake. I mean—"

Their conversation was interrupted as the hatch opened and the ramp slid down to rest with a soft thud on the hangar bay floor. Caitlin glanced at Marq once more, then turned toward the exit. She halted at the top of the ramp, taking a deep, shaky breath.

Marq went to her side. "I swear, I won't—"

"I know, I know. You won't let anything happen to me." She smiled at him and nodded.

"You must act the part. Say nothing. Stay close."

"I'll follow your lead," she said.

She was putting such faith in him. He wanted to hug her, to kiss her, but that would absolutely reveal his deception.

Instead, he headed down the ramp, relieved when he

heard Caitlin's steps behind him.

As expected, he noted more security personnel than standard arrivals dictated. They were most likely there to make sure that Marq was indeed the one returning with the skimmer.

He had hoped that Sorca would not be among them, but she stood near the landing pad, fists propped on her hips, the silver uniform tight enough to show the lines of her muscles even through its fabric.

The amber of her skin was washed out in the lights from the hangar, and her dark hair had golden streaks from her time on Earth in the sun. Her gray eyes twinkled with even more amusement than usual.

Marq felt his pulse quicken. He tried to calm his body so Sorca didn't detect anything amiss. She strode up to him with her relaxed gait, a broad smirk on her face as she looked at him, and then pointedly at Caitlin.

"Commander," Sorca said, though she was still looking at Caitlin. "Welcome back. I trust your trip to Earth was… vegeful."

"Vengeful?" Caitlin said.

Marq's stomach felt like it was collapsing on itself. Caitlin was already veering from their plan.

"Vegeful." Sorca stepped in front of the Earthling. "It's an Earth expression meaning that it was productive."

"I don't understand," Caitlin said.

"It's a metaphor. It means something like, 'I hope that

your trip provided sustenance in the form of plant-produced nourishment'."

Caitlin made a face, her head tilting as she sorted through whatever idiom Sorca's brain was twisting around this time. Understanding dawned—the crease in Caitlin's brow disappeared and her mouth dropped open.

"Oh, you mean *fruitful*," Caitlin said.

Sorca laughed. "What's the difference? It all beats nutrient bricks."

She nudged Caitlin playfully, which sent Caitlin staggering sideways into Marq. He caught her quickly, glaring at his security officer.

"Mind your strength, Sorca." Marq's voice had lowered. Even he could hear the menace in it.

He also realized he was holding Caitlin against his chest. He stepped back from her as soon as he was sure she had stabilized her stance.

Sorca's smile only grew. "Of course, Commander. And my apologies. I sometimes forget how much stronger my Cygnian DNA makes me when compared to other sentients."

Not other Sadirians. Other *sentients*.

Sorca knew. Moons, this could complicate matters.

He should have foreseen this. Sorca's bondmate, Eric, was an Earthling. With all the time she'd spent with Eric, Paige, and Evelyn while traveling to and from Sadr-4, she must have learned how to differentiate humans from

Sadirians.

"I'm happy to tell you I have nothing to report." Sorca emphasized the last word, then glanced over at her officers, dismissing them with a silent tilt of her head. "But know that I am available to you, as always, should you need... advice."

She winked at him, then turned and headed toward the exit from the hangar bay.

As soon as she was gone, Caitlin said, "Okay, she seems weird even by alien standards."

Marq gripped Caitlin's arm and led her toward the same exit Sorca had used. He leaned close, and said, "You'll need to watch what you say now that we're aboard."

"Right. No 'alien' talk, but— Oh...my...God!" Her voice rose on the last words—gaze locked on something above their heads. She seemed to be trying to muffle her volume, but ended up making a high-pitched, sustained "Eeeeeee" noise.

The remaining workers in the hangar turned toward Caitlin—including the pair of Antareans that she was staring at, wide-eyed, lips curled tight around her teeth and mouth clenched shut.

The Antareans were hanging from a coupling on the ceiling that only their species could reach without some form of antigravity lift or ladder. Ven, the *Reckoning*'s chief engineer, was scowling on a gravlift next to them, his arms crossed as he oversaw their work.

Antennae twitching in Caitlin's direction, the Antareans tilted their large heads from side to side. One of them lifted three of its arms and waved at her.

Caitlin kept making the sound, only quieter, as she slowly waved back.

Marq bent down and whispered, "Caitlin," in her ear.

"Sorry." Her voice was still a high-pitched squeak, but at least she stopped making that sustained sound.

Marq squeezed her arm gently as he guided her through the door.

This was going to be more of a challenge than he'd thought.

Chapter Eleven

"I'm so sorry, but what the heck even were those?" The muscles around Caitlin's eyes felt weird. Probably because she couldn't seem to shut them after seeing *giant ant people hanging from the ceiling.*

"Those were Antareans," Marq said. "They're helping my chief engineer, Ven, with some intricate repair work."

"Antareans. Like the ones who helped build that colony on the moon."

"Yes."

They had both been about her height, with slender reddish-brown bodies and watermelon-sized heads and eyes as big as grapefruits. At first, she'd been afraid they were going to drop on her and...eat her or something, but then she'd noticed that they had tools in their hands.

Or claws. What was the word for ant-hands? Had she learned that in her studies? It seemed like something she should know.

Her thoughts were racing. A shrill laugh bubbled up inside her, then spilled out.

She would have slapped her hand over her mouth to stop

it, but one was busy carrying her bag and Marq had a firm grip on the other. He used it to pull her into a smaller side corridor and spin her around.

He pushed her up against a wall, leaning in so close his breath rustled the loose hairs around her face. Her body immediately lit up, all the laughter and fear pushed away by the heat that welled within her whenever he was close.

"Caitlin, you've got to get yourself under control," Marq said. "You're going to see things on this ship that are unlike anything on Earth. If you keep having that kind of reaction, my crew will know you're not Sadirian."

"Kind of like how you reacted to my donkey?"

Marq let out a sigh, lowering his head. "I will protect you from physical harm, but there still may be consequences if you're discovered."

She let out an uneasy laugh. At least this time, she could keep the volume of the sound relatively low. "What, like space jail?"

He looked up at her, his gaze intense. "Like a mindwipe."

A chill swept through her that even his heat couldn't eradicate. Her imagination had managed to conjure up an image of her sitting in a chair with no memory of how to walk or talk or who she was or…anything. Heck, with this ship's technology, they might erase her mind and just stuff her into some sort of suspension tube to experiment on and

—

She stopped herself before she could freak herself out any more than she already had, and said, "You mentioned that when you were talking to Dane and Brigid earlier. What *exactly* does that mean?"

"It means your memory would be erased. Everything that's happened since just before I woke you up."

She would forget the amazing adventure her sister was having, and the fact that her twin had apparently found someone she cared for deeply. Caitlin would forget the amazing things she'd seen. The moon colony and the space station.

She'd forget Marq.

"What if I refuse?" She hated how small her voice sounded, but she already knew the answer.

"You won't have a choice. And neither will I." He leaned even closer.

"Just so you know, protecting my memories is just as important to me as keeping my body safe. And I expect you to keep your promise."

"I should have realized…" He shook his head. "I forget how different Earthlings are from us. Mindwipes have always been an accepted part of our culture."

"You're okay having your memories erased?"

"No, I'm not. This is more complicated than you realize." He glanced down the hall, then leaned closer, his voice barely above a whisper. "Sadirians sleep in regen beds to maintain our bodies in optimal condition. Dane and

I discovered that some regen beds have been integrated with technology from our programming chambers— devices that directly input the skills we need to complete our tasks, like languages and knowledge of various cultures."

"I really don't like where this is going," Caitlin said. Her stomach was in knots.

"Many Sadirians are programmed and reprogrammed every time they use their regen beds—their minds sculpted to best match our society's needs. Most aren't even aware of it."

"That's awful." She shook her head. A million questions lined up in her mind, struggling to escape all at once. "How invasive is the programming? Why haven't the people who know about this put a stop to it? Oh my God, is that why you'd never loved something before?"

"I was programmed to have my emotions suppressed, but Dane and I have worked to restore them."

"Marq." She didn't know what else to say. He was right. There was so much more going on here than she'd known.

"This is why you have to control your emotions. Many of my crew have gone through the same suppression program. Dane and I hope our work will help them should they decide to restore their own emotions."

"Did it work, then? For you?"

Marq laughed lightly and nodded. "It's taken a long time, but I believe it has."

"No wonder you were so freaked out before. This whole thing with Meredith must have been overwhelming."

"It was worth it to meet you. To experience this." He reached up and brushed a few stray hairs from her cheek. His thumb lingered, tracing her jaw, then down along her neck. His gaze heated.

The temperature seemed to jump about a hundred degrees. Once again, her body reacted instantly. Tingling energy rocketed through her belly and...lower.

"Stars, you're beautiful," he said.

Marq looked at her like he wanted to explore every inch of her body. He was leaning closer. So was she.

Using every ounce of willpower she hadn't known she possessed, she pulled back.

"If you want me to not show my emotions, this isn't the way to go about it," she said. "Because I guarantee that kissing me is going to get you a reaction."

His smile deepened as he shook his head. "You're right. I don't know what I was thinking."

She rested her hand on his chest, just above his heart. "You weren't thinking. You were feeling."

He let out a little laugh, then gripped her wrist and lifted her palm to his lips briefly.

"Are you going to be reprogrammed again if they find me here?" The thought made her skin break out in goosebumps—the unpleasant kind. She suddenly realized she would do anything in her power to protect him, too.

"I'm not going to let that happen to either of us." He gripped her arms and squeezed. "If we go through proper channels, there's a good chance you could join the Department of Homeworld Security. But proper channels do not include us being discovered talking about this in a corridor on my ship."

"Right. Sorry."

"Most of my crew is loyal to me, but there are some on board who would welcome any excuse to remove me from my position. I don't know who they all are."

No wonder Brigid had been worried.

"Can you control your emotions?" Marq asked.

Caitlin glared at him. "Sure."

"Commander?" A feminine voice carried to them from the main corridor.

Marq let Caitlin's arm go and stepped back quickly, turning toward the woman who had interrupted their moment. She had dark brown skin and her black hair was pulled into a bun. Some of the tight curls had escaped, and brushed across her forehead. Her full lips were pressed together tight as she tried to suppress a grin—and mostly failed.

"I've been looking everywhere for you." The woman held up what looked like a thin silver tablet computer and wagged it at him. "New requisitions, along with an update on our progress and some incident reports."

Marq's soft smile had been replaced with a grimace, and

the lines between his brows were back. For someone trying to not show emotions, he looked pissed.

He stepped toward the woman, his long strides bringing him close quickly. Caitlin fought another ridiculous surge of jealousy. The woman looked way more interested in Caitlin than Marq.

Marq took the device from her and started swiping the surface, staring intently at whatever it displayed.

"Contact with Earthlings is to be kept to a minimum," he said.

"I'm aware, sir." The woman was still staring at Caitlin, sporting a smirk she was no longer trying to hide.

"Nika," Marq said. "I'm not approving sandwiches from Buddy's House of Subs for you. It's enough that your team is receiving Earth-based rations."

"Well, you won't be getting my best work on *Outreach* station, then." Nika plucked the device from his hands. "Those sandwiches are inspiring."

Marq ignored her quip. "Send the full report to my quarters. I'll review it later."

"Of course." Nika's grin broadened. "I can see you're busy."

She turned and walked back toward the hangar bay. Marq headed in the other direction, and Caitlin hurried to keep up with him.

"Why can't she have her sandwich?" Caitlin asked, relieved to have a less-heavy topic to discuss.

"Nika's more interested in visiting Earth again than obtaining specific food," Marq said. "She didn't like being assigned to head the team building the space station, but she's the best engineer in the fleet. I need her focus here. The *Reckoning* has a supply of Earth rations now and has been incorporating it into our meal cycles. That should be enough for her."

"Is Brigid helping with that? Because I could totally see her coming up with a new fusion that incorporates your food with ours."

"We normally only eat nutrient bricks. I doubt she'd want to fuse that with anything."

"That sounds…" Caitlin wasn't sure what to say. It sounded awful, but she didn't want to offend him.

"Brigid called them *gross* and *boring*, if that helps." His smirk returned a bit as he glanced down at her, but disappeared quickly.

When they reached the end of the corridor, he waved his hand over an etched section of the chrome wall. It slid aside to reveal an elevator. Caitlin followed him into it, then watched as he started tapping on more controls.

The big ship had the same design elements as the skimmer. She'd expected more…variety, or something. The door *whooshed* shut, and she only had the vaguest sensation of movement.

"Can't you use your voice to control the ship?" she asked.

"We can. I just prefer the touch commands."

"So, you're a tactile kind of guy." She grinned at him. "Good to know."

His mouth opened, then shut, then opened again. Finally he looked away. His cheeks were a little pink.

"Are you blushing?" Caitlin asked in a teasing tone, sidling closer.

"Are you flirting with me?" He raised one eyebrow.

"Right. Sorry." Caitlin stepped away again, holding her bag in front of her with both hands and staring at the door. "You were totally blushing, though."

Marq laughed, and she realized it was quickly becoming her favorite sound in the universe.

Chapter Twelve

Finally, they were standing in front of the door to Marq's quarters. He sighed as he input the security code that would unseal his chambers, tension melting from his shoulders. The door opened and he gestured for Caitlin to precede him into the room.

"Wow, this is nice," she said.

To him, it had seemed like an opulent waste of space. After Meredith had moved in, and now knowing there were soon to be more cats in his care—not to mention having Caitlin with him… He was happy with the openness for the first time.

"Meredith is in here." He made sure the entrance to his quarters was secure, then crossed to his sleeping chambers. He opened the door and hurried in to check on his pet.

Meredith was curled up on the pallet where he normally slept, since he refused to use the regen bed attached to the side wall of the room. She had dragged over his spare uniform—the one he hadn't thrown into the cleansing unit yet—and made a small nest in it. Three little life forms were tucked in next to her stomach.

"Cygnus X!" he yelled. "They're already here."

Caitlin laughed. "I told you she knew what she was doing."

Meredith let out a chirruping meow, then stood and stretched. Marq gasped as the kittens rolled away from her body.

"Oh no." He dropped to his knees as he tried to determine how to help. He was afraid to touch the kittens—they were so tiny. He reached for them, but Caitlin grabbed his hands to stop him.

"The kittens are fine," she said. "But it's best if we handle them as little as possible at this age. And you should always wash your hands... Or decontaminate them? Whatever it is you do. Just do it thoroughly before touching them."

His heart seemed to stutter. Could he have injured them merely from his touch? Meredith circled, rubbing along his legs and sweeping her tail across him.

Caitlin pulled some sort of canister from her bag and sprayed a foaming agent into one hand, then returned the container to her bag and rubbed the foam over her hands. "Mama kitty needs some love."

"But she needs to tend to them." He gestured toward the kittens.

"Every parent needs a break from time to time."

Marq glanced at Meredith. As soon as he did, she stood on her back legs and propped her front paws on his thigh, purring and staring up at him with her large green eyes.

"I apologize," he said, sitting back so that he had a lap for her to crawl into. "This is all strange to me." He began to pet Meredith, being careful of…everything, since he wasn't sure how having kittens had affected her.

Caitlin dug through her bag again, this time pulling out a pair of blue synthetic gloves. "Babies are strange? Are you guys all grown in test tubes or something?"

"Maturation chambers."

She paused, one hand partially gloved, and stared at him. "You're kidding, right?"

"No."

She looked back to the kittens, blowing out a tense breath. "I'm going to process that…in a minute. Maybe fill me in after I've examined these little cuties." She smiled as she finished her statement, but he could see thin lines of strain between her eyebrows.

After donning her gloves, she picked up the first kitten —a white one with orange and black patches. The kitten's head was rounder than Meredith's, with the tiniest ears sticking out on either side. Its belly was impossibly big, and its tail miniscule. It let out a plaintive meow as Caitlin held it up.

The sound was barely more than a squeak, yet it felt as though Marq had been punched in the chest by a Lyrian.

"Is it distressed?" he asked.

"She just misses her mommy."

"*She?*" Marq could hardly breathe.

"Yup." Caitlin set down the kitten after looking it over, then picked up the one with matching fur patterns and began examining it. "Calicos are almost always female. That's what Meredith is, and these two girls have the same markings as their mom."

She set down the second kitten and picked up the one that was orange with white stripes. "Breeds are determined in part by their coats. This one is a marmalade tabby, and I'm guessing takes after their daddy." She looked it over, then set it down. "*He* certainly does."

She grinned at Marq, but then her smile vanished.

"Are you okay?" she said, shifting toward him.

"I'm fine."

"You're not fine. You look like you're about to pass out again."

"I'm perhaps…a bit overwhelmed. I have no idea how to care for them all."

Caitlin's gloves made snapping sounds as she pulled them off. She tossed them in her bag, then scooted over on her knees to sit next to him. She draped her arms across his shoulders, hugging him tight.

"I don't have any patients staying at the practice right now, and my next appointment isn't for a couple of days," she said. "I'll need to send word to my Aunt Renee so she can check on Bert and Ernie for me, but I can stay for a while."

Marq reached up and clasped her hand. "I would appreciate that a great deal. Would you also check on Meredith?"

"Of course." Caitlin turned back to her bag and retrieved a plastic pouch. She opened it, and Meredith immediately perked up.

"Oh yeah," Caitlin said. "You're feeling pretty good." She pulled a few small brown objects from the bag, then slowly lifted her hand toward Meredith. "And I know just how to make kitty-friends."

Meredith leaped from Marq's lap, almost scratching him in her haste. She sniffed at Caitlin's fingers for a moment, then grabbed the food Caitlin offered. Marq could hear a loud, distorted purr coming from Meredith as she chewed it. Caitlin ran her hands over Meredith's body, examining her.

"What is that?" he asked.

"Cat treats." Caitlin said. "I can leave you the bag."

"Thank you."

Marq wondered why Dane hadn't left any when he'd brought along the initial supplies for Meredith—food, toys, a litter box specially designed for use on a spaceship. Marq would have to ask when they spoke next.

Meredith returned to her kittens, curling up around them and grooming them with her tongue, as he'd seen her do to herself countless times.

Caitlin closed her bag and slid it next to the door, then

stood, offering Marq her hand as if to help him up. He took it, rising to his feet on his own.

"Your pets are fine," she said.

Marq let out a breath, feeling a bit lightheaded. "Thank you. That news is very welcome."

"Well, it's time to pay the piper."

She smirked, raising and lowering her eyebrows quickly. The expression was so comical, he found himself laughing. His reaction was no doubt influenced in part by his relief.

"Let's go sit on the couch so I can start interrogating you," she said, pulling on his hand.

"Of course."

He looked back at Meredith once more. She was already curled up with her eyes shut, her three little kittens nestled beside her. He pressed a command that would make the door to his sleeping chamber remain open, just in case they needed assistance.

Caitlin led him to the sitting area. She stood for a moment, staring out the viewports.

"It's hard to believe." Her voice was barely above a whisper. "So many stars. So much possibility."

He squeezed her hand, imagining her wonder. Sharing it.

"I'll tell you everything I can," he said.

"I guess you don't have to worry about telling me too much, since you can just erase my memory if you need to."

She started to tug her hand away, but he held on to it, turning to face her.

"I don't want you to forget me," he said.

She half-smiled. "I don't want to forget you, either."

Chapter Thirteen

Marq could never forget Caitlin. He doubted even a mindwipe would purge her from his thoughts. His chest tightened at the mere idea of anyone trying to take these memories from him, his heart racing.

Or perhaps it was her proximity.

She stepped closer, drawing one lush lip between her teeth and holding it there.

"You had questions?" he said, his voice lower than usual.

She nodded, but didn't say anything.

"What do you wish to know?" he prompted.

Caitlin laughed. "Everything. But we can start with this."

She placed her hands on his face and pulled him down for a kiss.

He didn't hesitate this time. All his doubts and fears and concerns had been eradicated.

Emotions were still new to him. But this he knew. The sharing of their bodies.

Gripping her waist, he crushed her against him,

devastating her mouth with his. His tongue plundered, his lips devoured. She was gasping when he traced a path along her jaw to her neck.

They stumbled to the hull and he lifted her from the floor as he had in her clinic and on his skimmer. She wrapped her legs around his waist again.

Even through their uniforms, the stimulation sent electric arcs of pleasure racing through his body. This time, he held nothing back as he moved against her.

"Holy crap," she gasped.

He reclaimed her mouth, matching his thrusts with his tongue, exploring her exquisite softness. When he pulled back, her expression was dazed, lips swollen from his kisses, her cheeks pink.

Wisps of dark silk floated around her face as her hair began to fall from its tie. He reached up and pulled it free while she collected herself, watching it cascade over her shoulders and rest upon her breasts.

"I need a minute to just…" She took a deep breath, then let it out. "I have a question."

Of all the times to begin her line of inquiry, she chose now?

Marq worked to hide his disappointment, trying to get his own breathing back under control. "Which is?"

"How do I take off your uniform?"

His cheek muscles twitched, a broad smile stretching them. And he laughed. A deep laugh that resonated in his chest and vibrated out to every limb.

He stepped back and let her slide to her feet, keeping his grip on her arms until she steadied herself. The moment she stopped swaying, she reached for the seal at the collar of her uniform.

"Okay, follow-up question," she said. "How do I take off *my* uniform? It kind of just hooked itself together when I put it on, but now it's stuck or something."

"Let me."

Rather than simply remove it for her, he gently grasped her hand and guided her fingers to her collar, showing her where and how to apply pressure to release the seals. Slowly, he drew her hand down her chest to open the uniform, letting their fingers brush the skin of her stomach as it was exposed.

The sight of her breasts pushed together in the too-tight underwear mesmerized him. He was surprised she'd managed to fit them into the Sadirian garment. He reached up and gripped the sides of her uniform, then pulled them farther apart so he could see more of her.

His dick pulsed insistently, almost painfully. He ignored it, focusing on the view before him.

Her skin was flushed, her chest rising and falling quickly with each breath. Her lips parted as she gazed up at him. He couldn't resist tasting them again.

He peeled her uniform down her arms as he kissed her, his fists tangled in the fabric. The softness of her skin was nearly overwhelming. He wrapped his arms around her, wanting to be closer, wanting to touch all of her and keep touching her forever.

Trailing his lips down her neck and across her chest, he pulled the top half of her uniform from her, then lowered himself to his knees. He finally willed himself to let go, but only so he could touch the velvet-smooth skin of her back as he kissed her stomach.

She grabbed the bottom of her undergarment and lifted it up and over her head, then tossed it away. Marq hissed in a breath as he saw it hit the ground.

If he looked up, he would lose control. Something about that particular part of her anatomy was hitting his system like a maxed-out plasma blast.

"I need to get some *Coupling*," he said.

"I think you meant, 'we need to get *to* coupling'." She laughed, tracing her fingertips through his hair.

He clenched his eyes shut, fighting the urges the intense pleasure brought forth in him. He pressed his forehead against her stomach. "*Coupling* is a drug we use to suspend fertility."

Among other things.

"I'm already on one of those," she said.

His surprise overpowered his self-control. He looked up at her, taking in the sight of her full breasts, rose-tipped nipples tight and beckoning.

"Cygnus X," he breathed.

"I don't know what that means, but from the look on your face, I'm guessing it means you're happy," she said. "So, fertility is taken care of. I get tested regularly and am all good, and you've already said you've been cleared of stuff that could be harmful to humans." She grinned at him. "This is the point where I would seductively unsnap my belt and step out of this outfit if I knew how to do that."

"Allow me."

He brought her hands to her belt, showing her the release points. His own hands were shaking.

Once the belt had released, he tugged her uniform down her legs, unsealing her boots so she could step out of them. That left her standing with only snug black undergarments clinging to her hips.

He reached for them, but she grabbed his hands.

"Nuh-uh. Now it's your turn." Caitlin stepped out of Marq's reach and crossed her arms over her breasts.

"Strip," she said.

He only hesitated a moment before pressing the releases at his collar that locked his uniform onto his body. As he stood, he said, "It's not often that I'm given orders."

"Because you're the Commander of the ship?" Her stare was intense as she watched him undress himself.

"Because I'm Commander of the *Reckoning*," he said, stepping out of his uniform and tossing it aside.

"Right. That's an intimidating name."

"It's an intimidating ship." He slid off his

undergarments and kicked them away, then stood and stared at her, waiting to follow her lead.

Her eyes widened, her gaze gravlocked to his groin. "That's not the only intimidating thing around here."

Chapter Fourteen

Marq was gorgeous. Broad, strong, muscled, with a fine dusting of hair. The sight of his hard shaft hit her like a bomb going off between her legs.

She could imagine how she'd have to stretch for him, how good it would feel when he finally sank into her. She quickly pulled off her underwear, staring at the muscles cording his thighs and the perfect lines of his calves.

Caitlin had never drooled over anyone before. Marq wasn't just anyone, though.

He was strong, sensitive, intelligent, commanding. She could see herself falling for him, hard. The way he was staring at her, she doubted she was the only one.

Then his lips were on hers again, crushing her mouth, demanding. One arm wrapped around her shoulders while he reached between her legs, cupping her sex. She gasped at his warmth, at the pressure of his palm in all the right places, sending searing blasts of pleasure along her nerves.

He kept on until the room seemed to spin around her, her body pulsing with energy too close to fruition.

"Marq," she said. "I can't wait any longer."

"Neither can I."

"You don't have curtains."

"What?"

"The couch is right under the windows. If someone flies by, can people see in?"

A small smile graced his lips. "The material is reflective. We can see out, but no one can see in."

"Good."

She grabbed his wrist to pull him toward the couch, turning to face the window and kneeling on the cushion. She looked over her shoulder to watch him approach—tall, ripped, and exuding a confidence she hadn't seen earlier.

A heady feeling washed over her as she remembered his words, the way he'd looked at her, the way he was looking at her now.

She looked back out the window, at the endless stars and her own translucent reflection staring back. Marq appeared over her shoulder. The cushions sank as he knelt behind her, his thighs spreading her legs.

His hands touched her next, one splayed over her belly and the other cupping her breast. Heat, longing, and pleasure pounded through her, her heartbeat drumming in her ears. She was trembling, she wanted him so badly. She felt as though her body might unravel at any moment from the intensity of it.

The hand on her belly slid down to the dark curls between her legs. She felt his dick at her core, then parting her, filling her.

Her eyes drifted shut as she turned her focus inward, savoring the pleasure pulsing along her nerve endings, but only for a moment. She didn't want to miss anything with him—anything about this incredible experience.

He pulled himself almost out, then slid back in, their bodies rocking together. She braced her arms on the back of the couch, trying to hold off the energy that was blooming inside of her as she met his strokes.

His thrusts grew stronger and faster, the pressure within her built. Her blood felt like fire, her skin electrified.

"Caitlin," he gasped, grabbing her hips and drawing her back against him to match his near-frenzied movements.

The energy she'd been keeping at bay exploded, flowing along her saturated nerves, melting into her muscles, drowning out all thought and reason except for this moment of perfect pleasure.

He finally stopped, his shaft buried as deep as possible in her, chest plastered against her back, sweat-slicked bodies not even letting air between them.

His breath fanned her neck as he lowered his head next to hers. She wasn't sure where she began and he ended.

This wasn't just pleasure. It was something more. Something she'd never experienced before.

Unity.

Chapter Fifteen

The universe was filled with miracles. Caitlin was absolutely one of them.

Marq didn't want to part from her, to end this moment of absolute and complete bliss.

This was the first time he'd partnered with someone without using *Coupling*. The experience was exquisite.

"Is this what it's always like?" He breathed the question into her ear and kissed her neck.

He felt a tremor ripple through her body. Felt it everywhere they touched.

"Never," she said. "At least, not for me."

He felt the truth of her words as soon as she uttered them. This wasn't just the lack of using the Coalition drug. This was him and Caitlin.

She shifted forward and he finally let himself fall back, parting only long enough to sit next to her on the couch and draw her into his lap. She leaned against his chest, but didn't say anything. Didn't even look at him.

"Is something wrong?" he asked.

"No. Yes. I don't know."

"I'm confused."

"Me, too." She twisted around so that she was straddling him, giving him ideas should she decide to couple with him again. "I want to kiss you."

He smiled and leaned forward. "By all means."

She pressed her fingers to his lips, pushing him back against the cushions. But then, she moved her hands to cradle his face and bent to kiss him. A light, lingering kiss that stirred something in his chest. A tightness whose origins he couldn't fathom.

When she pulled back, he said, "Now I'm even more confused."

She laughed. "Sorry about that."

"Never be sorry for kissing me." He brought his hands to her hips, then ran them over the smoothness of her bottom.

She pulled in a hissing breath between her teeth and leaned forward, pressing her breasts against his chest. His body began to stir again, surprising him.

"This is crazy," she said. "You make me crazy."

The tightness in his chest increased. "I... That sounds like a bad thing."

"I don't know. This is so intense and fast."

"Should we have waited before coupling? I thought it was what you wanted."

"It was...is...and feels like it always will be. And that's freaking me out."

He parsed through her words, trying to understand her concern. Only one theory made sense, and his heart picked up at the mere thought of it.

"You wish to pairbond with me," he said. "To become my bondmate."

It would solve so many of their problems—protect her from a mindwipe, give her the ability to be aboard his ship, give him clearance to visit her on Earth.

"Whoa, whoa, whoa." She shook her head. "That would be absolutely insane."

His heart felt like it had turned to lead in his chest. He would need to visit the medbay if these vacillations continued.

But then, she pulled her lip between her teeth and held it there.

A slow smirk pulled on his face. He could feel it.

She wanted the pairbond. She just didn't want to admit it.

"Stop looking so smug," she said. "This isn't *just* because you're that good in bed. Even though you are."

"I don't understand," he said, though it was an idiom he actually knew. He feigned a confused expression. "We've only been together on the couch."

She let out an aggravated growl. "We have known each other for like four hours. Even *I* am not that impulsive."

"Pairbonds aren't permanent," he said. "They can be dissolved."

She looked stricken. A furrow appeared between her eyebrows and her mouth dropped open for a moment, before snapping shut.

He hurried to reassure her. "But only if you wanted that," he said. "I can't imagine not wanting more of this."

She arched an eyebrow, but was still frowning. "I guess it was good for you, too, then."

"It was amazing. Like every moment with you has been."

At last, she smiled. "This has been the greatest adventure of my life."

"Then let it continue."

Her smile broadened, the corners of her eyes crinkling. She leaned in and kissed him. Marq wrapped his arms around her, feeling the heat of her skin against his, the warmth of her heart.

She pulled back after a few long and wonderful moments, resting her forehead against his. "I hope we'll still feel this way when the adrenaline wears off."

"I have no doubt of it." He kissed her briefly. "Whatever lies before us, we'll face it together. Being with you makes me feel that anything is possible."

Chapter Sixteen

Caitlin stretched and cast a lingering look at Marq as he slept. She wanted to check on the kittens again, and honestly, for all their super-advanced technology, the Sadirians sure couldn't make a comfortable couch. The foam pallet he'd laid out in the other room looked worse—even if it hadn't been occupied by Meredith and her kittens.

Comfort didn't seem to be that important to Marq's people. He didn't have any blankets and there was no oversized T-shirt for her to pull on.

If she was going to be sticking around—and she really, really wanted to stick around—she'd talk to him about making some changes. Not just for her, but for his entire crew.

"Blankets and sandwiches for everyone," she whispered.

Marq had left the door to the other room open. Caitlin stepped inside and was immediately greeted by Meredith lifting her head and letting out a trilling purr-meow.

"There's my happy mama," Caitlin whispered, dropping to her knees beside the cat and her family.

Caitlin scratched behind Meredith's ears and petted her,

feeling her ribs and stomach more out of reflex than any concern. The kittens stretched and rolled over, getting comfortable in their cozy bed.

"At least you guys look comfy. And you, Miss Meredith —you get a lifetime of cat treats for introducing me to Marq, you little matchmaker."

Meredith half-rolled over, giving Caitlin better access to scratch under her chin.

"And lots of lovin's."

Caitlin laughed, trying to keep her voice low so she didn't wake Marq. In the stillness of the rooms, she easily heard the soft *shoosh* of the door to Marq's quarters opening behind her. Meredith perked up, eyes wide and pupils dilating.

Caitlin stopped herself just in time to keep from asking aloud if this was someone Meredith knew. Something in the cat's posture put her on alert.

Standing as quietly as possible, Caitlin inched to the door and peered around the corner.

"It didn't have to come to this, Commander."

A man was standing between her and Marq—the repairman from the hangar bay.

Ven?

Ven's right hand was fisted and pointing toward the couch as his left hand hovered over his bracer. Marq was propped up on one arm. His eyes moved to her, but the rest of him was unnaturally still.

Caitlin started to step forward, but Marq's eyes narrowed ever so slightly. She ducked back into the room where she was hiding.

Why the heck hadn't she taken the time to get dressed before checking on Meredith?

"The High Council will rise again," Ven said. "And when they do, those of us who remained loyal will be rewarded."

Her heart started to pound. Ven was one of the bad guys?

"Craaaap," Caitlin mouthed, looking around the room for something to use as a weapon. Her gaze fell on her medical bag. She knelt next to it, digging through its contents as quietly as she could.

Cat treats, deworming medicine, stethoscope... There it was!

She lifted the vial of tranquilizer and grabbed a syringe packet. She winced at the noise it made when she ripped it open, holding her breath. Ven was still talking in the other room.

What was the dose needed to knock out a Sadirian? Would it even have the same effect on them as a human? What if Ven had a reaction and it killed him?

Her options were limited, and she—and Marq—were in danger.

Caitlin filled the syringe with an amount that would incapacitate a human in seconds, but not kill them. The similarities between humans and Sadirians better be more than skin deep.

Crouching at the door with her weapon in hand, she realized she had another problem. How to cross the room to him and inject him before he noticed her.

Marq was still frozen in place. She remembered him holding his arm up toward Bert back on Earth, hand fisted in the exact same manner as this guy. Marq hadn't had his uniform on then, but it had seemed a reflexive action.

Maybe Ven's bracer was doing something that was paralyzing Marq. Marq had said the bracers could do amazing things—things he'd disabled in her uniform for her and everyone else's safety.

Ven had better hope this effect was temporary. She didn't need fancy technology to mess him up.

"This planet has a corrupting influence on our people," Ven said. "It will be purged and stripped of resources, along with anyone who sides with them. This is your moment to choose."

Ven slid a finger over his bracer. Marq shook his head, then tried to lean forward. His neck strained with effort, but no other part of his body moved.

"What kind of stasis field is this?" Marq said.

"One developed for the High Council's interrogators."

"An interrogator?" Marq glared at him. "That wasn't in your personnel file. How many agents of the High Council are left aboard my ship?"

"Not *your* ship," Ven shouted. "This is *Teisha's* ship. And she will be restored to her place the moment we finish our work here."

Caitlin modified her grip on the syringe, placing her thumb on the plunger so she could inject the tranquilizer as soon as she stabbed the needle into Ven's body. She took a deep breath, rallying her courage, and prepared to creep into the room.

A small form darted between her legs, nearly tripping her.

"Meredith," she whispered.

Luckily, Marq shouted, "Meredith!" at the same time, covering the sound of Caitlin's voice.

Ven jerked away from the cat as she ran up to him, yowling, hissing, and swiping at him with her claws. He turned his bracer toward her.

"Oh, no, no, no!" Caitlin rushed out from her hiding place, holding up the hand with the syringe and roaring at him as she did. She had no idea what he had planned for Meredith, and wasn't about to wait around to find out.

In other circumstances, the look on Ven's face would have been hilarious. Caitlin hoped she'd have a chance to look back on the entire ridiculous situation and laugh.

Ven's eyes widened and his jaw dropped open. She wasn't sure which was freaking him out more—the yowling cat or the screaming, naked Earthling charging at him.

There was no way Caitlin would reach him in time. He was already bringing his other hand down on his bracer's controls and had lifted it toward her.

For a brief instant, Caitlin was grateful that Meredith at least wasn't in immediate danger. Then Marq slammed into Ven's side, tackling him to the ground.

Ven swung at Marq, his fist connecting with the side of Marq's head. The blow didn't faze him. With barely a pause, Marq grabbed Ven's wrists, trying to pin them.

Ven twisted away from Marq's grip, elbowing Marq in the jaw hard enough that his head snapped back. As Ven pressed his advantage, Caitlin saw her chance.

She leaped forward, grabbing a fistful of Ven's hair. Without hesitating, she stabbed the syringe into his neck and pressed the plunger in one panic-stricken movement.

Ven lurched to his feet, hitting Caitlin with his back and knocking her into the wall. She smacked her head on the metal, then slid to the floor, the lights flickering in her vision.

"Caitlin!" Marq charged forward, slamming into Ven's stomach with his shoulder and lifting him from the ground. Ven flew across the room, then landed in a tangle of limbs on the floor.

Marq paused, his chest heaving, staring at Ven's still form.

"Did I kill him?" Marq said.

"No." Caitlin held up the syringe. "Donkey

tranquilizers, remember?"

Marq stared at her for a moment, then he laughed. A full, deep laugh.

Caitlin joined in, but then the adrenaline hit her system. She started to shake, tears streaming down her cheeks even as she continued to laugh.

Marq rushed to her side and dropped to his knees beside her. He wrapped his arms around her and buried his face in the nape of her neck.

Meredith leaped onto his back, staring down at them from over his shoulder and making chirruping noises. She curled her feet under her body and closed her eyes as if this kind of thing was absolutely normal.

Caitlin let out another laugh as Marq kissed her neck and held her tighter.

They were safe—at least for now.

Chapter Seventeen

"The search you ordered after the attack revealed a number of explosives on the *Outreach* station and in *Kindred* colony." Nika's gaze remained fixed on Caitlin and Meredith sitting on the couch together while she gave her report. "There were none in the mining colony, as you expected."

"Of course not," Marq said. "The Sadirians still loyal to the idea of the High Council want to use the mining colony to take Earth's resources for their own ends. Why redo the work we've already done, especially with Vegan technology integrated with our own?"

Nika arched an eyebrow at him, then crossed to the couch. There had always been an empty corner created by the positioning of the furniture in his sitting area that bothered him. He'd found a use for it now.

Nika peered into the space and said, "This is an interesting use of Earth resources."

Marq had ordered that his and Caitlin's Earth clothing be brought from the skimmer to his quarters at Caitlin's request—after they'd donned their Sadirian uniforms once more. Soon after the Earth clothing arrived, Caitlin had piled the material in the corner beside the couch.

Meredith had moved her kittens to the new location almost immediately. He was happy to have his pets closer, yet now they were revealed for all who visited him to see.

It was only a matter of time.

"The explosives were placed recently," Nika continued. "This was a well-planned attack. Ven couldn't have been acting alone."

"I never thought he was," Marq said. "We need to search through the personnel files again."

Nika nodded. "Sorca can also talk to soldiers we knew were opposed to the High Council before it was destroyed. Maybe they've heard something."

"If they had, they would have come to me," Marq said. He'd connected—very discreetly—with several Sadirians among the ranks of the *Reckoning* who'd also learned of some of the High Council's reprehensible acts and shared his desire for change.

"You sure about that?" Nika smiled at Caitlin. "You've been a bit…distracted lately."

Caitlin shook her head. "Don't look at me. I only just got here."

Nika laughed. "I was talking about the cats. Does Sorca know about these? I don't recall them being scanned and cleared to come aboard."

Caitlin snorted, then said, "We call that an import

quarantine." She must have realized her mistake, because she quickly added, "When we're using our Earth-human words."

Both Nika and Marq stared at her.

"You really need to work on your girlfriend's vernacular if you want anyone to think she's one of us."

"What?" Caitlin looked at Marq, her eyebrows furrowed. "I'm Siberian. No, wait, that's a husky…"

"The word you're looking for is Sadirian." Nika reached over and scratched Meredith's chin. "And you're not fooling anyone."

Caitlin's shoulders slumped. She stared at Meredith and stroked the cat's fur.

"Don't worry about it," Nika said. "Most people on board won't be paying attention, especially if you stick with the Commander."

Caitlin cast her a weak smile.

"Caitlin won't be on the *Reckoning* much longer," Marq said. "She's a doctor who tends to a wide array of Earth animals. Her expertise is needed on her homeworld."

"Thanks." Caitlin's words were flat, her expression guarded. Had he offended her somehow?

"Are you the only veterinarian on Earth?" Nika made a circle with the fingers and thumb of one hand. "Because *we* have zero."

"I've checked out Meredith and the kittens and they're fine." Caitlin stood with Meredith and crossed to Marq, handing him the cat. He held Meredith close, comforted by her presence. Caitlin wrapped her arms around his elbow and leaned against him. Warmth spread through his chest.

This was how he was meant to exist. Caring for Meredith with Caitlin at his side. He could feel it in every fiber of his being. It was as though they were already becoming a unit. A *family*.

"I have a lot to learn about all this," Caitlin said.

Marq nodded. "We all do."

"I'm just not sure I'm qualified," Caitlin said. "I mean, I take care of animals."

"And I have a feeling there will be more of them on our ships and in our colonies and space stations." Marq glanced over at Nika, who was standing on her tiptoes to get a better view of the kittens over the edge of the couch.

"You're right about that," Nika said. "Ever since Lily joined the Department of Homeworld Security, Ari pretty much always has a different cat in his arms when I see him. He's obsessed with the things, same as Cyan." Nika walked over to them and gestured to Meredith. "Is that where you came by this one?"

"I actually don't know where Meredith is from," Marq said. "Dane snuck her on board."

Nika nodded. "Well, now that they're here, I have a feeling others are going to want their own as companion animals. I could just see these little guys climbing the trees in *Kindred* colony."

"That might not be such a good idea," Caitlin said. "Cats are notorious for getting in places they aren't supposed to."

"Which means they'll be more likely to need a doctor to tend them from time to time." Nika smirked at her.

Marq set Meredith down and watched as she trotted back to the corner to check on her kittens. When she was settled, he turned to Caitlin and took her hands in his.

"I wouldn't ask you to give up what you have on Earth," he said. "But if there's a way we can work together—can *be* together—I would like to find it."

"I'd like that, too," she said.

Nika cocked her head. "Okay, then. I'll inform the Department of Homeworld Security that we're bringing on a new member and leave you two to sort out…the logistics." She waggled her eyebrows at Marq.

"You should tell them in person so you can swing by that sandwich shop you like so much," Caitlin said.

Nika smiled. "Oh, we are totally keeping you."

"That's not—" Marq said.

"Too late." Nika threw her hands in the air and hurried to the door. She exited into the corridor, yelling, "I'll bring you back a cookie."

As soon as the door had shut, Caitlin laughed and said, "I like her."

Marq's mind was filled with so many scenarios, infinite possibilities that alternately terrified and exhilarated him.

He wasn't sure what path Caitlin would want to take.

"You can speak freely now," he said. "If this isn't what you want—"

Caitlin grabbed his face in both hands and pulled him down for a kiss. He stepped closer, pressing her body against his, deepening their connection.

At last, they parted, though she stayed close.

"I want to be part of this," she said. "I want to be part of you."

The room seemed to spin around him, his body as light as if the gravity generators had failed.

Now more than ever he was sure they would find a way to make this work. The new Coalition, the alliance formed by the Department of Homeworld Security.

Peace in the galaxy. *Real* peace that all sentients worked to achieve and maintain of their own free will.

A future with Caitlin.

He pressed his forehead to hers and said, "Then so be it."

Epilogue

Nika didn't waste any time prepping a skimmer for her trip to Earth.

She would swing by the Florida base first and tell them about Caitlin and Marq's cats. Ari would want to see the kittens immediately. He might even commandeer Nika's skimmer, stranding her on Earth.

Darn.

And, of course, while she was there, she'd need to eat. She grinned as she input her route and initialized the launch sequence.

The landing gear retracted into the ship, leaving the skimmer hovering in the hangar bay. This was always her favorite moment—the ship suspended, as if holding its breath right before beginning a new adventure.

Then she was out of the bay, stars streaming past. She wished she had time to take a more scenic route, but she was still kind of worried the Commander would call her back. She missed Earth too much to pass up a chance to visit it again. It was the only place that had ever felt like home.

Plus, Buddy was there.

Her stomach did flips as she thought about him—and not because of his amazing sandwiches. It was his smile, the way he laughed, how he listened whenever she went on about an engine, even though he had no idea what she was talking about.

Which was a good thing.

Her smile dimmed.

She was an alien. Earth might feel like her home, but it wasn't. After she finished building *Outreach* station, she'd probably be reassigned halfway across the galaxy.

Her skills were needed, she knew that. But her best work came when her heart was in it.

And her heart was on Earth.

The skimmer banked, heading toward the darkened hemisphere before her. Toward the planet that had given so many of her friends new lives unlike anything they could have imagined.

"Please," she whispered. "Just one more miracle."

—

Thank you so much for reading *Import Quarantine*! I love the new direction the series is taking, with more time coming up on ships, space stations, and the lunar colony. The next adventure takes an unsuspecting Earthling far from home—and during the Winter Holidays, no less! Read on for an excerpt.

Homeworld for the Holidays

The Department of Homeworld Security
Book Twelve

Chapter One

Winter

Everything was perfect.

Buddy stepped onto the sidewalk, surveying the work he'd done in his front yard. Lights twined around the orange tree and hugged the branches. A "Santa and his

Reindeer" that was almost life-sized filled most of Buddy's yard, surrounded by other holiday figures. Every edge of the house itself was outlined in multi-colored lights.

He'd skirted close to going overboard, but thought he'd pulled off the right balance. Now he just needed the guest of honor.

On cue, headlights cut across the seashell-and-asphalt road. Nika pulled up in her sleek silver truck, her eyes wide as she stared out the window. The *closed* window.

For such a state-of-the-art vehicle, it never made sense to Buddy that the windows didn't open. Nika had explained once, talking about AC efficiencies and techno-stuff he didn't understand, but what if she wanted fresh air?

The night was chilly, adding a crisp snap to it. At least, as close to a crisp snap as they could get in Florida. It was one of the few reminders that today was the first day of Winter.

"Get it together, Buddy." He smiled and waved at Nika as she stepped onto the sidewalk, then slowly closed the door behind her.

"Wow," she said. "This is…"

"I wanted to surprise you." He approached, turning to gesture toward his display when he reached her. "What do you think?"

Her eyebrows were high on her forehead. The multicolored lights cast a rainbow glow on her brown skin and reflected off her dark eyes—the warmest eyes he'd ever looked into.

"I think it's a lot of lights," she said.

"Well, it's Christmas. I mean, almost. I don't want to presume about how you celebrate the season, so that's why I invited you over today."

"What's today?"

"The Winter Solstice. I figure, as much as everybody does their own thing, we can all agree that today is the first day of Winter." He quickly added, "In the Northern Hemisphere."

"I didn't know people celebrated that," she said.

"People celebrate all kinds of things. What about you? What's your favorite holiday of the season?"

"I've never actually celebrated anything."

"Wait, like...ever?"

She thought for a moment, then said, "There was that special sub you made me after I fixed your deep freeze. You said that was something to celebrate."

"Yeah, but that's... I'm talking about holidays. You've never celebrated a holiday?"

She shook her head.

"Not Christmas or Hanukkah or Kwanzaa or... anything?" he asked.

She raised her arms slightly, then let them drop back to her sides.

"That's kinda...rough." He ran his hand over the back of his head, ruffling his hair.

"But this is beautiful." She gestured toward his house and took a step closer to him. "I'd like to learn more about it."

Buddy could feel that he was grinning like an idiot, but couldn't stop himself. Nika did that to him. No other woman had ever gotten to him like she did.

He had friends who chose not to celebrate holidays for various reasons, but for them, it was a choice. He'd already figured out that Nika's childhood had been beyond sheltered. She didn't get the simplest expressions, sometimes. It was almost like she was brought up on a different planet. But at least she was trying to broaden her horizons.

"Where do you want to start?" he asked.

She strolled around the Santa, but stopped on the other side of the sleigh and gazed up at Buddy with a questioning look.

Of course, she'd go to the vehicle first. She was a mechanic, and near-obsessed with her job, from what he could tell.

"Old St. Nick," Buddy said. "Good idea."

He walked closer and gestured toward the sleigh. "Santa is popular with the kids. He travels around the world on Christmas Eve, flying in his magic sleigh pulled by these here guys." Buddy patted the closest reindeer on the flank, careful not to knock it over.

"The sleigh… flies," she said.

Buddy nodded. "Uh-huh."

"Not because of an engine, but because it's pulled by animals. Who can presumably also fly."

"That about sums it up. Oh, and Santa delivers presents to all the little girls and boys who have been good that year," he added. "Squeezes down the chimney and puts them under a tree we bring inside and decorate for the occasion."

Nika arced a single eyebrow at him. How could she have not heard of Santa? He had to fix that, to share what he could of the childhood she'd been denied.

"I remember one year, I stayed up till midnight and snuck into our living room to see Santa." Buddy smiled as a wave of nostalgia swept through him. "My dad was putting presents under the Christmas tree. He'd dressed up in the costume and everything. But he couldn't resist the cookies mom and I made, and he had to pull down his beard to eat them. When I saw him, I freaked out. He and mom made me promise not to tell my sisters, but I was wrecked the next day."

Nika's eyes widened again. "You believed the story was true?"

"Sure I did. It was a big part of the magic of my childhood."

"And he's part of this Solstice celebration?"

"Not exactly. He's more tied in with Christmas, which is what my family celebrates. We'll have a big get-together in a couple days at my Aunt Verna's place."

And if he could work up the nerve to ask, Nika would be there as his guest.

"There are so many celebrations and holidays around this time of year," he said. "I didn't know which one you observe—or, I guess, don't observe, so... This..." He shrugged. "This is just for us. You and me, together on the Solstice. A new tradition."

"Oh." Her lips tightened in that way that let him know she was trying not to smile. And failing.

He circled around the sleigh until he was standing right in front of her. Taking her hands in his, he walked backwards, leading her toward the house.

"Come on inside and see the tree," he said.

"The tree that you brought inside your house so the made-up man can put presents under it."

Buddy cocked his head as he nodded. "Well, yeah. But it's so much more than the story. It's the memories you make and being with the people you..." His mouth went dry and he stopped, staring down at her.

Say it, Buddy. Come on now.

He opened his mouth, but all he could manage was, "Care about."

Dammit.

Nika smirked up at him, as if she knew what he'd been trying to say. He sure hoped she did, because at this rate, he'd never be able to say the words.

Normally, he was so smooth around women. They would practically throw themselves at him.

Nika was different. He knew she was into him, but she held herself back. She held herself back from everything, as far as he could tell. Everything except her machines. And maybe his sandwiches.

They'd been hanging out as his sub shop for months now. The more time they spent together, the more he liked her.

And the more he had to lose if he accidentally chased her off.

Aside from his family, he'd never told anyone he loved them. Nika was the first person he'd wanted to. He had all night to work himself up to it.

He angled his head toward the house. "It might not get too cold around these parts, but the humidity makes it go straight to your bones. I have hot cider mulling, and I made us a special dinner."

"You're always cooking for me." She stepped a little closer and interlaced their fingers.

His heart started to race. "I have to make sure you keep coming back, don't I?"

"Buddy, that's not the only reason I visit."

"I know." That goofy grin came back with a vengeance, pinching his cheeks almost. "It's also because of my dog."

She busted out laughing, as he'd hoped.

"Pickles is a big motivator," she said. "But that's not

what I meant."

He took a deep breath, even though his chest felt full as they smiled at each other for a quiet moment.

"Listen, Nika." His heart was pounding. Moment of truth time. He could do this. "We've been friends for a while now. I was thinking…maybe we could be—"

Her watch let out a piercing beep.

Something more, he finished in his head.

"I'm sorry," Nika said. "I have to take this."

Buddy sighed and nodded. They'd been through this before.

"I get it," he said. "It's okay."

"Buddy…"

"No, really. I get it. Your work is important."

"So are you." She let out an exasperated grunt as the beeping intensified.

He stepped away and rubbed the back of his neck as she looked at her watch. He wasn't sure where she'd picked it up, but it seemed much more advanced than other smart watches he'd seen—a perfect match for the smartest woman he'd ever met.

"Crap," she said. "They need me at… At the garage. It might not take long. I can try to come back later tonight."

"Yeah?"

"Yeah." She smiled, but her eyes were pinched around the edges. "I want to taste that dinner you made me."

—

About the Author

USA Today Bestselling author Cassandra Chandler uses her vivid imagination to make the world more interesting, spawning the ideas she turns into her whimsical Science Fiction romcoms and darkly evocative Paranormal and Urban Fantasy Romances. Fast-paced and funny, lighthearted or dark, her stories will introduce you to characters you want to be friends with and worlds where you'd like to build a vacation home.